I opened _____ _____ and stared at the _____ _____ _____ _____ blinds. All I could think about was Matt. Was he up yet? Was he angry? Sad? Did he ever go back on stage and perform?

I thought about calling him, but I knew he wouldn't talk to me. Rubbing my eyes, I kicked off the covers and sat up. I could e-mail him an apology. I crawled across the bed, turned on the computer, and rubbed my hands together and yawned. What would I say?

Sorry. Sorry that I kissed another guy in front of you. Sorry that I tried to make you jealous. You see, I was just trying to save our relationship.

Yeah, right. That would work.

5

TURNING
seventeen

Can't Let Go

by Rosalind Noonan

A PARACHUTE PRESS BOOK

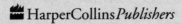
HarperCollins*Publishers*

Created and produced by
PARACHUTE PUBLISHING, L.L.C.
156 Fifth Avenue, Suite 302
New York, NY 10010

Published by
HarperCollins*Publishers*
1350 Avenue of the Americas
New York, NY 10019

First HarperCollins*Publishers* printing, December 2000

HarperCollins® and 📖®
are trademarks of HarperCollins*Publishers* Inc.

Library of Congress Catalog Card Number: 00-100944
ISBN 0-06-447241-8

Printed in the U.S.A.

10 9 8 7 6 5 4 3 2 1

Design by AFF Design
Cover photos by Anna Palma
Hair and makeup by Julie Matos for Oribe Salon

Chapter 1

My heart pounded wildly as my boyfriend's lips touched mine. For a minute I completely forgot that we were sitting in his car outside the apartment building where I lived. I just closed my eyes and kissed him.

"Mmm." I sighed as his fingers brushed the tender skin at the back of my neck. Sometimes I still couldn't believe that Matt Fowler was *my* boyfriend. Sure, I'd dated lots of guys, but Matt was different. He really understood me. And okay, he was gorgeous. Piercing blue eyes. Wavy brown hair. A totally athletic body from playing wide receiver for the South Central Lions.

I wanted to keep kissing him, but Matt pulled back. "Hold that thought till we get upstairs," he said as he turned off the engine of his Jeep.

"Right." I jumped out of the car and tugged on my backpack. "Race ya!" I cried, and ran toward the apartment building.

"No way! You have a head start!" Matt shouted as he charged behind me.

Ever since football season ended, this was our after-school ritual. Matt would drive me home and hang out at my apartment for a while. My mom worked as a junior-high guidance counselor and usually got home a few hours after us.

"Gotcha!" Matt rushed up the stairs and gave me a huge bear hug as I keyed my way into the apartment.

I turned in his arms to hug him back. "Yeah, but I let you catch me."

"You always do that. It's no challenge at all. Now a two-hundred-pound linebacker, that's a challenge." He lifted me off the ground and hauled me into the apartment. I laughed as Matt kicked the door closed and gently tossed me onto the couch. "So . . . where's Dan?" he asked.

Wiggling out of my backpack, I glanced toward my brother's room down the hall. Dan was twenty years old and had quit college to start a business online. At the moment his old bedroom was his headquarters. I usually could tell if he was home by the monitor glow (or lack thereof) coming from his room. "No glow," I replied. "He must be out."

A dark curl fell over Matt's forehead as he flashed me a conspiratorial look. "Does that mean we're actually *alone*?"

I gazed at Matt and smiled. "So what do you want to do?" I asked, nuzzling and kissing his neck.

"Let's celebrate with a double bacon cheeseburger," he replied.

I pushed him away. "You're kidding, right?"

"Uh-huh," Matt pulled me closer and kissed me passionately on the lips. Then he stopped.

"What?" I asked.

"Well, now that I mentioned it, I *am* kind of hungry."

I sighed and got off the couch. "Okay," I said, going into the kitchen. "But that would be minus the bacon and the burger. Mom purged the fridge of meat a few weeks ago when she went through that whole macrobiotic thing."

"How could I forget?" Matt asked, peering into a fridge filled with tofu and vegetables.

I glanced at the counter and noticed the stack of letters and ads on the table. "Dan must have brought in the mail," I said. I was leafing through it when I saw a familiar seal on a return address. "Oh, my God."

Matt placed a small container of soy milk on the counter as I stared at the crisp envelope.

3

"University of Miami?" he read aloud. "Whoa. Do you think it's about your scholarship?"

"I don't know," I said nervously as I ripped open the envelope. I had received an early acceptance from Miami, but I'd been waiting to hear about a scholarship. The Witker Grant. Mom planned to pay my tuition, but there was no way she could afford all the other costs: room and board, books. . . . I really needed that grant. If I got it, I could go to the school of my dreams. If I didn't, my life was pretty much over. "This is it—my whole destiny, folded in this thin envelope." I winced, turning it in my hand. "Shouldn't it be fatter? Filled with forms and stuff?"

"That's the rule for admissions letters," Matt said. "Scholarships are different, I think." He touched my shoulder. "Go on, read it. I'm sure you got it. Who could be more perfect than you for that grant?"

My hands were shaking as I took out the few pages and unfolded the cover letter. My eyes skimmed the first few lines. "Thank you for applying . . ." I read aloud. "Looking forward to seeing you in September. . . ." My heart pounding, I skipped ahead. "Unfortunately, scholarship funds are limited and we received an overwhelming number of qualified applicants this year. Thus the

4

University of Miami is unable to offer you the Witker Grant at this time." I collapsed onto a kitchen chair. "They turned me down."

"It's not so bad. It's just for the scholarship," Matt said sympathetically as he rubbed my shoulders. "They still want you. They even sent forms for you to sign up for room and board."

"But without that grant, I can't *afford* room and board." I tried not to sound whiny, but it's hard to be upbeat when your dreams are slipping through your fingers. "I can't believe it. I wonder if I can appeal to the committee or something."

"Who knows?" Matt sat down beside me and reread the letter. "You should ask your mother."

"Mom!" I snapped my fingers. Of course. Guidance and counseling were her business. "Great idea." I grabbed the phone and hit the speed dial to her office. She picked up the phone, and I launched into the whole sad story. "Do you think if I write a letter they'd reconsider?"

"Oh, honey . . ." Mom said, her voice heavy with that I-feel-your-pain tone. "I wouldn't waste time on an appeal. They've already given that grant to another student. What you need to do now is refocus your energies."

"On what?" I asked. Collecting loose change? Cashing in bottles?

"On other colleges," Mom replied. "I told you to apply to a couple of safety schools. Places we can afford." She paused. "You have a week or two before most colleges stop accepting applications. Why don't you concentrate on that—before it's too late?"

Because I don't care about other colleges, I thought. *I've found the perfect place for me, and now I just need the money to go there.* I bit my lip before I could snap back at Mom.

"How about I bring home some more catalogs? I'm sure there's a less expensive school with a good physical therapy departement," Mom added. "I didn't want to burst your bubble about Miami, but it's been weighing on me ever since I had that astrology reading. You're a Virgo—that's an earth sign. Miami is basically a water place. The ocean, the bay, the canals. I'm just afraid that your Virgo soul would be unhappy surrounded by all that water. Maybe you should think about a school here in the Midwest."

"Mom . . ." What could I say? That my Virgo soul longed for a wild college beach party? Not that it was the only thing drawing me to Miami, but it was just as rational as choosing a college by your astrological sign. "I wonder if there are some water signs in my chart," I said. "But we can figure that out later. 'Bye, Mom."

Matt looked up from the scholarship rejection letter as I hung up. "So no go on the appeal?"

I shrugged. "She wants me to apply to other schools. I'm not interested."

"And you didn't fight with her about it?" His blue eyes flashed as he smiled at me. "I'm impressed."

"I don't want her to feel bad. I mean, she works hard. It's not her fault she can't afford the U of Miami on her own. She's done everything alone without help from . . ." I paused, not wanting to get into the whole subject of my father again.

After my parents divorced when I was seven, my dad moved to Arizona and disappeared from my life. It was pretty devastating to lose him, but it was even worse when I found out that he moved back to Wisconsin years ago. He'd been living in Milwaukee—less than two hours away—and he'd never even bothered to see me. He tried e-mailing me a few months ago, but I cut that off as soon as I figured out what a liar he was.

"The single-parent thing," Matt said. He poured two glasses of milk and slid one over to me. "I give your mom a lot of credit for that. But what about applying to other schools? I hear Purdue is great . . . for football."

I laughed. The joke was on Matt, whose parents pushed him to apply for a football scholarship at Purdue, where his brother was a hotshot player. Matt was worried that the time spent working out and studying with the team would consume every minute, ruining his chance at studying his real love: music. Matt played jazz guitar.

"Oooh!" I stood up and paced across the kitchen. "Is this as hopeless as it feels?"

"No, not at all!" Matt insisted, waving the embossed letter from the U of Miami at me. "You'll find a way to get the money by September. In the meantime, you just have to make sure you get this room deposit in on time."

"Deposit?" I nearly croaked. "Room deposit?" I took the letter from him and read:

If you wish to secure a room in a University dormitory for the upcoming academic year, you must submit a deposit of $1500.00 to the University Bursar's Office postmarked no later than Thursday . . .

I looked up from the paper. "Thursday? As in less than two weeks away?"

"It *is* a tight deadline," Matt agreed. "I guess they want to see who's serious about attending."

"Well, I'm seriously screwed," I said. "I mean,

there's a chance I'll get some other scholarship money from the university, but that won't happen until sometime in the spring. Without the Witker Grant I'm stuck for that deposit. I know. I'll get Dan to buy some more lottery tickets for me. What are my chances of hitting the big jackpot before the deposit is due?"

Matt got up from the table and put his arms around me. "Don't worry, Kerri. We'll figure out something."

I leaned my head against his shoulder. "Okay, but let's think about it later. Right now I just want to feel sorry for myself for a second."

He hugged me, then leaned back. "Time's up."

"I feel better already," I said. Matt downed the rest of his soy milk, then went into the living room and grabbed his backpack. "Hey, are you out of here?" I asked him.

"Major calculus homework," he said. "I'm gonna squeeze out a few problems before the game. Pick you up at seven?"

Although I was glad for an excuse to spend Friday night with Matt and my friends, I wasn't in the mood to cheer anyone on. "Right now cheerleading at a basketball game is like the last thing I want to do. I'd rather take a calc final. *Two* calc finals—with a broken pencil."

9

Matt leaned in to kiss me good-bye. "Be back in a few hours."

"Can't wait," I said as he headed out the door. "And we're going out afterward with my friends—if that's okay. I hope it is, 'cause it's all planned," I called after him.

"Sounds good," he said.

I shut the door and headed to my room. Maybe checking my e-mail would get my mind off the fifteen hundred dollars I had to raise in less than two weeks.

When I logged on to my computer, I saw that I had two messages. The first one was from Maya Greer to Jessica Carvelli, Erin Yamada, and me. The four of us were best friends.

> **Just a reminder that you're all coming to my house for a sleepover tomorrow night. Last-minute addition to the party list—Amanda. Knew you wouldn't mind. Other addition—Marlene. Well, not to the party, but she'll be at the house. I mind, but Dad doesn't get it. See you at the game tonight.**
>
> **XXXOO, Maya**

I could picture Maya at her computer, her heart-shaped face pinched with anger as she typed in a few digs about her father's new girlfriend.

Maya's mom died two years ago from ovarian cancer. I could only imagine how hard it must be for Maya to get used to Marlene and her fifteen-year-old daughter, Amanda. Marlene kind of expects Amanda and Maya to be instant best friends. Weird.

I clicked Reply All and started to type the news about the University of Miami. But after starting five different sentences, I stopped. Everything I wrote sounded so pathetic. Poor, pitiful me. Maybe I was feeling that way, but this was just a temporary setback. It had to be.

Outside my room I heard the door open. "Is that you?" I called, figuring it was Dan.

"No. Just a burglar," came my brother's voice. I ignored him. Not hard to do, since I knew he'd immediately park himself in front of his PC. The only good thing about having Dan around was that he'd insisted on having two telephone lines so that we could use the phone and the computer at the same time. Works for me.

Clicking back to my e-mail, I saw that the other message was from my father. Gag. I clicked Delete without reading it. Then I checked to see if any of my friends were online for an instant chat. Nope.

I pushed back my chair. Time to grab a

sandwich if I was going to cheer my heart out at that basketball game.

Dan was sitting at the kitchen table, his blond, stubbly hair glistening in the fluorescent light. I glided past him and grabbed the bread from the counter. The bag was open. Only the heel was left. "Did you rush home just so you could ruin my dinner?" I asked, shoving the bag aside.

"Sorry," he said.

I turned around to face him. It's not like my brother to apologize for anything.

"About this." He was staring at the letter from Miami. "Accepted but no way to pay. Sort of like a collegiate Cinderella."

"That's mine." I snatched the letter away from him. "Isn't it against the law to read someone else's mail?"

"The law doesn't apply when it's left sitting on the kitchen table." He pulled the crust from his sandwich. "I believe that's called the kitchen table exemption."

"It's called none of your business," I said. "And I am going to Miami, by the way. I'll come up with the money."

"How? By juggling bagels at Bernie's?" He snorted. "Did the minimum wage go up to a hundred dollars an hour?"

"And when was the last time you saw a paycheck? I don't see any money flying out of that computer in your room."

"New businesses take a while to get off the ground," Dan replied. "Bill Gates didn't make his first million overnight."

"Bill Gates didn't start his business in his mommy's apartment," I said, grabbing a pot from the cabinet and filling it with water.

"Ouch." Dan grinned. "For that, you're not getting any stock options when the business takes off." He took a sip of water from the glass on the table. "What's the big deal about Miami, anyway?"

"They've got exactly what I want." I placed the pot on the stove and turned on the fire. "One of the best physical therapy programs in the country."

"Come on," he said. "Other schools teach physical therapy. You're looking for an escape. I saw the brochures."

I braced myself against the stove as the images from the University of Miami catalog danced through my head. Sunny beaches. Palm trees against a backdrop of blue skies. Beautiful tanned guys and girls. It was all so un-Wisconsin.

"So what if I want to get out of Madison?" I admitted. "All of my friends are leaving, and I'm not going to be left behind. Stuck in my room." *Like you, Dan,* I added silently.

"Well, you'd better buy more lottery tickets," he said. "A lot more."

"Already thought of that." I pulled out four dollar bills from my pocket and handed them to him. "Get me four for tomorrow."

Dan tucked the money into the pocket of his T-shirt. "A few more bucks down the drain."

"You know, you're no help at all."

"Ah, but I could be," he said. "I have the answer to your dilemma."

I folded my arms. "No, I am not investing in your company."

"You always assume." He shook his head. "But I have something even better. I know someone who can pay your college room and board."

It was too good to be true. Nothing is ever that easy. But my brother was chewing his sandwich with such a smug, knowing expression, I had to ask him. "Who?"

Chapter 2

"**D**ad can help you pay for college," Dan said.

His answer made my stomach twist. "Just tell him to make the check out to the bursar's office," I said sarcastically. Sometimes my brother can be a pain, the way he tries to play with other people's feelings. I grabbed a box of spaghetti off the counter and poured some into the boiling water. "It's not going to happen," I added.

"I wouldn't rule it out if I were you," Dan said. "Especially if you're serious about going to Miami. I happen to know that Dad is feeling guilty about ditching us. He wants to help."

"Well, for someone who wants to help, he sure doesn't show it," I said. "How do you know all this, anyway?"

"E-mails. How else?" Dan folded his arms. "I've been in touch with him over the last few months. No big deal."

Maybe not for you, I thought, remembering the turmoil my father had caused me a few months ago. It was Dan who'd found Dad's e-mail address. It was Dan who'd given Dad my e-mail address. Thanks for nothing, bro.

I stepped back from the stove. Remembering the whole thing almost made me lose my appetite. How Dad and I e-mailed each other. How I let myself believe he wanted a relationship. And how I found out the truth—that he didn't want me showing up at his doorstep, so he lied about where he was living. Was he lying when he said he thought about me all the time? Probably. It hurts so much that I almost wish I was still in the dark about my loser father. I grabbed a wooden spoon from a drawer and stirred the boiling pasta. Then I pointed the spoon at my brother. "Why are you doing this, Dan? Why do you have to keep bringing him back into our lives?"

"I'll let you in on a little secret." He glanced toward the front door, as if Mom was going to pop in at any minute. "Dad gave me some seed money for the business."

"What?" I almost dropped the spoon.

"Okay, it was just five hundred dollars," Dan admitted, "but it was what I needed. And I didn't have to see him or sign away shares to my computer business or anything."

"Dad gave you money?" It was hard to believe. I frowned at Dan. "He gave you money, and you didn't *say* anything?"

He shrugged. "It didn't involve you."

"I am so mad at you!" I turned back to stir the boiling spaghetti again.

"You'll get over it," he said. "Especially after you get the money from Dad. You don't know it, but I just made your day. Maybe your year."

"And you didn't meet with him? Did you at least talk to him on the phone?"

"Yeah, once or twice. But you know . . . I'm not into that interpersonal relationship stuff." He grinned. "Besides I didn't want to see him. I just wanted his money."

"Right." My brother had all the charm and social skills of a worm.

"I've got his address and phone number. I'll e-mail it to you."

"Thanks a million," I said sarcastically as he went to his room, leaving a balled-up napkin and a plate of crumbs on the table.

I spooned out a strand of spaghetti from the pot and blew on the steam. My brother was whacked, no question about that. But I couldn't help wondering what if. What if I found my father? How would he act when he saw me? What if I told him about my college expenses? What if . . .

"Action, action, we want action!" I shouted from the sidelines of the basketball court in South Central's gymnasium. I kicked in the air and then twirled, finishing the cheer.

In the stands students and parents clapped along, trying to push our players to score. We were trailing Lakeside High by six points, and the game was totally dragging. I spun back to my original position and caught Matt's eye. There he was in his usual spot: sixth row, off to the right with his friends from the football team.

Matt nodded and mouthed, "Sloooooow game."

On the court one of South Central's players got the ball and pressed forward. Pushing myself, I followed the head cheerleader's calls and tried to give the game my all. When the final buzzer went off, I didn't know if we'd won or lost—I just wanted to cheer that the game was finally over.

The players disappeared into the locker rooms, and everyone else spilled out onto the gym floor.

Matt was by my side in a flash. "We are so lucky Washington came up with that hook shot at the end."

I linked my arm around his waist and leaned

against him for support. "Yeah. Does that mean we won?" I asked.

"Hey, Kerri! Wait up!" someone called from the bleachers. I spotted Maya waving from the top row. She flipped her long brown hair over one shoulder so she could navigate the steps. Her boyfriend, Luke Perez, was following behind her. My other friends, Jessica and Erin, were already leading the way down.

Erin was the first to cut through the crowd and stomp across the gym floor. A boxy black wool coat swirled around her legs as she strutted, revealing the brightly colored strips of fabric she had sewn around her black flowing pant legs. Add to that her exotic eyes and raspberry-streaked black hair, and there was no doubt about it: Erin had an intrinsic sense of style.

"Can I tell you? Organized sports are just not my thing," Erin said as Jessica and Maya joined the group. "I just spend the whole time checking out the uniforms and wondering if there's a reason they're so dorky."

Jessica nudged Erin. "Yeah, right. I was sitting beside you, and you weren't watching uniforms."

Maya laughed. "We were rating the players. Butts to struts."

"Let's not go there," Matt warned.

"Yeah," Luke agreed. "We don't want to hear it."

"And what's up with you, Kerri?" Jessica said, her dark eyes studying me. "Not that you didn't cheer fabulously, but you weren't your usual high-energy self."

I frowned. "I was hoping it wouldn't show."

"Only to someone who's known you since kindergarten," Jess said. "What's wrong?"

"It's about the University of Miami," I replied, trying not to let the awful feeling inside me slip out. Somehow, if I admitted that I was scared, it seemed to make the possibility of not going to Miami that much more real. "I got a letter from the scholarship committee," I said casually. "They didn't give me the grant I was counting on."

"No way!" Erin cried.

"And you worked so hard on that essay," Jessica said. "You were in seclusion for an entire week."

"It's so unfair," Maya chimed in.

"Those committees are ruthless," Jessica added. "And we're still in the thick of it. Admissions forms, interviews, essays. At least you know you're accepted, Ker."

"But without that grant I don't know how I'm going to pay for it," I explained. "And there's a room deposit due in, like, two weeks."

"This calls for a full-fledged brainstorming

session," Erin said. "If anybody can come up with a plan, you can, Kerri. And we'll all help you."

"We can talk about it at Bernie's," Maya said, looking through the thinning crowd. "But I'm supposed to bring Amanda to my house later. Anyone see her?"

We all looked around.

"Isn't that her on the top bleacher?" Luke asked. He pointed to a petite girl with short blond hair. She was curled up with her knees to her chin, talking a mile a minute to a surrounding group of boys and girls—sophomores, from what I could tell.

Maya nodded. "I'll give her a few minutes, then go grab her and we'll all meet at Bernie's," she said.

"Not me," Luke told Maya. "My grandmother's visiting, remember?"

"I know, I know." Maya planted a kiss on Luke's lips.

"See you guys later." He waved and headed out of the gym.

"'Bye, Luke," I said as a couple walked up to our group. It was Erin's next-door neighbor, Glen Daley, and another senior girl who looked familiar.

"Yo, Yamada," Glen teased Erin. He and Erin were next-door neighbors. "I thought you avoided sports events and all things that ooze testosterone."

"I came for my friends; I stayed for the dirty-water dogs," Erin replied. "What's up with you?"

"Tiffany's brother used to play for South Central, so she's still pretty tied in to the team," Glen said. "We're heading out to a party at Tom Lander's house if you guys are interested."

"We've got plans," I said, worried that everyone would choose partying over solving my dilemma.

"Whatever," Glen said, "but if you change your mind, you're all welcome."

"Thanks anyway," Erin said as Glen and the girl walked away.

"Who *is* that?" Maya asked, staring after them. "Tiffany?"

"We met her at the New Year's Eve party, remember?" Erin answered. "Glen's really into her, but I think she's all wrong for him. It won't last."

"Not if you have your way," Jessica muttered.

Erin turned to Jessica. "What is that supposed to mean?"

Uh-oh. I thought. *Here it comes.*

Jessica's eyes narrowed. "What is with you, Erin? Do you enjoy going around and breaking up other couples, or are you practicing to be the anti-Cupid?"

Erin blinked, obviously stung by Jessica's remark.

For a minute none of us said anything. We all knew why Jessica was so angry at Erin. It happened at Matt's New Year's Eve party. Jessica had just told us she was getting back together with her old boyfriend, Alex McKay. Then Erin commented about how Jess had been dating this college guy behind Alex's back. But Erin didn't know that Alex was standing right behind her. It was an ugly scene. In the end Alex called it quits with Jess. Finito forever.

"Take it easy, Jessica," Erin said carefully. "I was just making an observation."

"Really?" Jessica pulled on her ski jacket and started zipping it up. "Funny, but that wasn't what I saw. I saw two people who . . . who seemed happy together." She choked a little on the last part of the sentence, and suddenly I knew what she was thinking. She was thinking about how happy she'd been with Alex at one time.

"Jess . . ." I moved away from Matt and touched her arm, but she couldn't look me in the eye. I think she was afraid she'd start crying. I wanted to make her feel better. I also wanted this tension between Jessica and Erin to end.

Jessica took a deep breath, and the awkward moment was over. "Let's get going," she said. She turned away and nudged Maya. "Would you tell Amanda we're out of here?"

"See you at Bernie's," Maya said, heading across the gym toward Amanda's crowd. "Come on, Erin."

But Erin didn't follow her. "You guys go without me."

Jessica kept walking, but Maya paused and called back. "You sure? We need your brain."

"Positive," Erin told Maya. Then she turned to me. "I'll give you some gray cells tomorrow. Since I'm here, I want to head over to the auditorium. There's a rehearsal going on tonight. It's a new show."

"Hey, don't bag out because of Jess," I said. "She's got to get past that thing about Alex—and will."

Erin tossed her head as if the whole scene hadn't fazed her. "Nah. I just remembered Mr. Calvert saying he could use some help tonight."

I grabbed my jacket and bag from the girls' locker room, and Matt and I headed out into the cold night. The minute Matt slid into the driver's seat, I reached over, put my arms around him, and planted a big kiss on his cheek.

Matt pulled me closer, and I felt myself melting in his arms. "I could tell your heart wasn't in it tonight."

His words gave me a warm feeling inside. *He understands me,* I thought. *He knows what I'm going through with this college thing, and he cares.* "There should be a rule that you can take a game off when you get totally unfair news from the college of your choice," I said.

"Yeah," Matt said, his blue eyes sparkling in the moonlight. He studied my face for a moment, then looked away. "I have to be honest. I know you're really disappointed about not getting that grant, but it made me wonder. I mean, college is just months away, and if you go to Miami, we're going to be, like, a thousand miles apart. Did you ever think of that?"

"Well, not exactly," I said honestly. "When I looked at colleges, I was thinking about other things. A good physical therapy program. A cool place to be. Nice weather. You know, all the stuff that sort of leaps out of the catalog photos and says, 'This is where you'll be happy!'"

Matt nodded. "When I first hit on the Web site for Boston College, I was convinced. This is the place. Now I just have to convince my parents. But . . . " He lifted my hand and gently kissed it. "I'm really going to miss you, Kerri."

"Me too," I said in a hoarse voice. All the time I'd been mooning about that scholarship money, Matt had been thinking about how we'd be apart. At that moment I loved him more than ever. This time when I kissed him, he kissed me back and gently stroked my hair.

As the kiss ended, I slid one hand inside his

jacket. Underneath, his chest was warm and solid. "It's not like anything has to change between us. Let's figure out how we're going to see each other next year."

Matt pushed my hair back and kissed my neck. He kissed my chin. "A plan is good, but right now I just want to be here—with you."

"Now that I'm thinking about it, if we don't have a plan, the soonest we'll see each other is winter break."

He kissed my ear. "I know. But we're together now. Can't we skip the plan and jump on the moment?"

"Jump on the moment," I repeated, smiling. I pressed my nose into his thick hair. The smell of his shampoo softened the cold air. "You're right," I said. "I wouldn't want to miss the moment."

"Good." He lowered his face close to mine. "Then kiss me again."

Chapter 3

"Okay, let's try to be professional about this," Jessica said, putting down her mug of decaf.

We were all settled around a low table at Bernie's Bagels surrounded by overstuffed furniture. Amanda was curled up in a big chair. Maya and Jessica shared a sofa, just across from the couch Matt and I were on. Jessica pushed her mug aside and slapped a pad of paper onto the table. "We need to come up with a bunch of ideas, a whole list of things that Kerri can pursue to get the money she needs for the University of Miami."

"The Kerri Hopkins Scholarship Drive," Matt said, sprinkling cocoa onto the foam of his cappuccino.

"I've got an idea," Amanda piped up. "How about stripping? I hear lots of girls do it to pay their way through college."

"Why didn't I think of that?" I replied. "The

money is great, the costumes are cheap, and it's so warm in Miami that I wouldn't worry about being cold." I caught Maya and Jessica staring at me as if I had two heads. "Uh, *kidding*!"

"Hey, you never know," Maya said with a smile.

"Miami is so far away, Kerri." Amanda took a nibble from her brownie. "What made that school your first choice?"

"It's my *only* choice," I answered. "That's why I went for early admissions. Now that I know I'm in, I don't have to apply anywhere else."

Maya gave a mock shiver. "No safety school? How many times did they tell us? Apply to at least three schools. One dream, one practical choice, one safety net."

"You know Kerri," Jessica said. "She's all or nothing."

"Yeah, but why Miami?" Amanda asked.

I shrugged. "When I saw the brochures, I just got a feeling that this place is my destiny."

"All those tanned bodies and sunny beaches," Maya said. "Not a bad destiny at all."

Amanda started laughing and almost choked on her brownie.

"But you're missing the point," I told them. "It's about physical therapy. You guys probably don't remember, but when I was little, I was in a car accident with my mom."

Jessica nodded. "When you hurt your knee. I went with my mom to visit you in the hospital. We were kids then, maybe five or six."

"I don't remember that." Maya blinked. "You never talked about it either."

I hesitated. I hadn't thought about the accident for years, not until guidance counselors started asking questions about real careers: What did we want to do after college? I guess in the back of my mind the answer was always clear.

"I barely remember the surgery," I said. "But after the operation I needed physical therapy. The doctor even warned my mother that I might not be able to participate in sports when I got older."

"He was definitely wrong about that," Maya said.

I nodded. "And every time I run by Lake Mendota or go to a cheerleading competition, I think about my therapist, Kathy. She made getting better fun. And I'll never forget her for that."

"That's an awesome story," Amanda said. "No offense, but I never thought a cheerleader could be so deep."

"Our Kerri is just full of surprises," Maya said, pretending to wipe away tears.

"Hello? We're getting off track here," Jessica said, reeling us in. "We're supposed to be thinking of ways for Kerri to pay for school."

"Maybe you should write up that physical therapy story and sell it to a producer or something," Amanda said. "It sounds like a great TV movie to me."

"Oh, right," I said, rolling my eyes. "And Britney Spears can play me."

"It's an idea," Jessica said, scribbling on her pad. "And right now we can't afford to rule out anything."

"Have you thought about a student loan?" Maya suggested.

Matt nodded. "One of my buds who graduated last year—he borrowed thousands of dollars, no problem."

"That's scary," I said. "But there's a cap on those things. I'll probably take a loan, but they're not going to let me borrow the kind of money I need. Besides, it's not going to help me pay for this room deposit. Fifteen hundred dollars in two weeks."

"Is Dan's business making any money yet?" Maya asked. "He might be able to help you out."

I let out a breath. "Dan's not making any money, at least not from what I can see. But he did try to help. He told me I should contact my dad in Milwaukee and ask *him* for the money."

I expected to get a laugh, but I didn't.

"I must have missed this part," Matt said,

picking up his mug. "Was Dan serious?"

"Dan says that our father is feeling guilty, and he wants to help. And paying my room and board will be a big help."

"I think that's a great idea," Maya said. "After all, he *is* your father."

Not really, I thought. Okay, maybe according to biology. Beyond that we had no relationship.

"I don't know . . ." Jessica pursed her lips. "Are you sure you want to do this? I mean, what if you're just chasing an image of a dream father?"

Her words stung me. I was talking about getting money for college, not capturing a father. But instead of snapping back, I tried to cover my feelings with a joke. "Oh, no!" I let my head drop onto Matt's shoulder. "I'm being psychoanalyzed by a coffeehouse shrink."

"Kerri . . ." Jessica lowered her voice and leaned toward me. "Remember how excited you were when your father started e-mailing you? But he wasn't at all like the guy you remembered. A father who—"

"Come on, Jess. Save it for a psych class." I tried to sound light, but I felt myself getting defensive. She was pushing too far. And she was wrong. "Look, I'm just telling you what Dan said. I'm not going to contact my father." I thought about it for a second. "But if I *did* get in touch with the guy, *not that I ever would*, I'd do it for one thing and one thing only—college money."

Jessica nodded. She took a sip of her decaf. "Uh-huh. Right, Kerri."

"What?" I asked, a little annoyed. She was staring at me as if she didn't believe a word I was saying. "You think I *want* to see him?"

Jessica didn't reply. She just eyed me with that knowing look of hers.

I stifled a comeback. I had no intention of meeting with my father. Of all people, Jessica should have known that. But now I caught myself thinking about it. Would he be glad if he saw me? Maybe not thrilled, but what about just a little happy?

"Well, you would have to get in touch with your dad soon," Maya said. "Considering that you have less than two weeks to come up with the room deposit."

I wanted to point out that I wasn't going to see him at all, but again, something held me back. And Maya was right about one thing: I didn't have much time to come up with that money. As I cradled my coffee mug, I couldn't help wondering what would happen if I actually did go to my father for help. Would he want to patch things up and contribute to my college fund? Was it possible that after all these years my dad might be the one to fix this huge problem for me?

Matt turned to me. "You're not really thinking about it, are you?" He paused, then fell back against the sofa. "You are. You're totally thinking about it."

I nodded. After all, where else was I going to get fifteen hundred dollars in less than two weeks? Somehow I didn't think asking for a raise at Bernie's was going to cut it. And the likelihood of my winning the lottery was pretty much zilch. I had to be practical about this. Going to my father was the only *real* chance I had of getting the money. "I need to do it soon," I murmured. "I'm free tomorrow." A little laugh slipped out. Was I crazy? Maybe. But sometimes you have to go a little nuts to keep your sanity.

"You're serious about this?" Matt asked.

"Why not? Milwaukee isn't far. Less than two hours." I picked up my mug and looked around the group. Suddenly a wave of fear rushed through me. Maybe this wasn't the best idea. Lots of things could go wrong. *Don't back out now, Kerri, just because you're a little scared*, I told myself. *It's your best shot at going to Miami*. Then I took a deep breath and smiled at my friends as if it was no big deal. "Anybody up for a road trip tomorrow?"

Chapter 4

"I can't believe you're driving to Milwaukee in the morning," Matt said as he steered his Jeep into the parking lot of my apartment building. "I mean, if you could wait a few days, I could probably go with you."

"I wish you could," I said. "And I wish Jessica didn't have to study for an exam tomorrow too. But Maya can go, and I'm going to call Erin when I get home. I just don't want to wait—or I'm afraid I'll change my mind."

I noticed that my mother's car wasn't in her reserved spot. "Hmm, Mom's not home," I told Matt. "She must be out with Yucky Chucky." Aka Chuck Berman, Mom's way-too-young-for-her boyfriend who has this greasy, stringy ponytail that really gets on my nerves.

"Really?" We got out of the Jeep and hit the stairs. "That means we're lucky for two reasons. No chance of seeing the Chuckmeister, and we finally get the living room to ourselves."

Exactly what I'd been thinking, but I slapped Matt's sleeve just to give him a hard time. Tonight we didn't do our usual race up the stairs. Matt just followed me quietly. When we reached the door, he put his arms around me.

I sighed, loving the way he felt. "It's definitely not a good idea for me to go to Milwaukee without you." I ran my fingers over the light stubble under his chin. "Actually, it's a terrible idea. Not just the Milwaukee part."

"I know." His eyes softened. "The dad part, right?"

"Bingo," I said, and admitted how nervous I was about meeting my dad. "But I can't do what Dan did. I can't just take money from my father without seeing him. And I know I play the tough act when it comes to my father, but the more I think about it, the more I'm afraid that he won't want to see me. Or that he won't recognize me or remember me."

"Who could forget you?" he teased. Matt cupped my head in his hands and stared into my eyes. "You're going to be fine, okay? You'll be back in a few hours, right? By this time tomorrow it'll be over. We'll be together, laughing about it."

"Oops." I winced. "Not tomorrow night. I mean,

we won't be together. There's a sleepover at Maya's."

"Hey, let me psych you up for this trip, okay?" Matt teased.

I couldn't help but smile. He was doing his best to get me out of this funk. "Sorry, coach."

"This time tomorrow the worst part will be over. And you'll tell me all about it on the phone. And we'll laugh over how you were so nervous. Still nervous?"

"I'm okay. If only my knees would stop shaking."

"Your knees will be fine," he said. Now his voice wasn't so authoritative, but tender. "I promise."

We kissed again. A more passionate kiss, and I felt his tongue moving over my lips. The breath caught in my throat as he pressed me against the door to my apartment.

Then the door opened.

I gasped and nearly stumbled out of his arms. My mother stood there, looking as surprised as I felt. "Mom . . ."

"I thought I heard someone out here," my mother said, bending down to move the welcome mat. Not that it needed straightening.

"Mom, your car isn't in its spot," I blurted out.

"It's in the shop," she said. "The transmission again. How are you, Matt?"

"Fine, Liz. I was just heading out." He dropped his arms from around me, then looked back at her awkwardly.

"Okay, then. Good night." Mom went inside but left the door cracked open.

Matt let out a breath, almost laughing. "How embarrassed am I?"

I smiled. "Well, now I guess I have to go inside."

He nodded. "Good luck on the Milwaukee trip."

"Shh!" I glanced behind me. I didn't want Mom to know about my plan. After the way Dad hurt me back in September, I wasn't sure she'd let me drive to Milwaukee. This trip was going to fall under the "don't ask, don't tell" rule.

"Call me tomorrow night?" he whispered.

I nodded. "And for Sunday . . . let's plan something."

"How about a run in the morning?" Matt asked.

Matt ran all year, even in the snow. "Okay," I said. "A run, and then we can go for coffee." I stood on my toes for one last kiss. Then I started counting. "If we meet Sunday morning, that's thirty-four hours." I glanced at my watch. "Thirty-three hours and fifty-nine minutes . . ."

"So how do you feel?" Erin asked me as we drove over to the Castle the next morning. That was our nickname for Maya's enormous house. "Are you nervous? Excited? Feel like you're gonna puke?"

"All of the above," I answered. I'd woken up anxious and spent most of my energy trying to deny the fact that I was nervous about seeing my father. I packed everything I needed for the sleepover at Maya's. Then I told my mother I was going for a drive with the girls. I didn't want to talk about Dad with her—or with anyone right now. Including Erin.

"Did you bring your maps?" I asked to change the subject. "You have to navigate. Maya's not good at that. She thinks east is always to the right."

"Got 'em. And I have directions from the Web. Takes us straight to the address you e-mailed me: Caswell Lane." Erin leaned back and propped her purple combat boot on the dashboard. "I'm just glad Jessica is too busy to grace us with her presence. Can you believe the stunt she pulled last night?"

"Weird, I know. But she's still upset about Alex."

"And still blaming *me* for the fact that they're not together," Erin added. "I mean, I apologized to her only like a thousand times. She's being totally unfair."

"I know, I know," I said as we pulled onto the lakeside drive leading to Maya's house. "She's got to put the whole thing with Alex behind her. But you know, it's not like Jess to hold grudges. Give her time. She's a totally loyal friend."

Erin pulled off her tie-dyed wool cap and twirled it around on one hand. "Funny, but it doesn't *feel* that way."

Up ahead loomed the massive house where Maya lived with her dad, with its stately pillars and sprawling green lawn. Maya said the shrubs around the house kind of looked like a moat. Ever since then we've been calling the place the Castle. I pulled into the circular driveway, spotting another car there. Two people were just getting out.

"It's Marlene and Amanda," Erin said. "On Saturday morning? Maya's right. Marlene is always here."

"Yeah," I said, watching as Marlene got out of the car. She primped her curly brown hair, then waved to us.

"They might as well just move in," Erin added.

"The press would have a field day with that," I said. Maya's father, currently a district attorney, was running for lieutenant governor of Wisconsin. The media featured him all the time, and the *Madison Herald* even printed a story about Maya recently, just because she was stopped by the police for trespassing. It was so unfair, but since Mr. Greer was into politics, Maya had no choice but to deal with it.

I was going to shut off the engine and go

inside, but Maya popped out of the house. Her tan shearling jacket was open, and her backpack dangled from her shoulder. She waved to Marlene and Amanda, then ran over to my car and pulled open the passenger-side door. "Hey, chicks!" she said. "Let's go before Marlene grills me."

Quickly, Erin swung her boots around to get out and let Maya into the backseat. But not fast enough.

"Maya!" Marlene called. "Where are you off to?"

"Milwaukee," Maya answered. I would have kicked her if she had been in kicking range. Didn't she have the sense to make up a story about our road trip?

"There's an exhibit at the museum there that we're supposed to see for school," Maya went on. Well, at least she lied when it counted.

Marlene's eyebrows rose. "What exhibit is it?"

When Maya looked lost, Erin jumped in. "It's a collection of Expressionist artists."

"Really?" Marlene seemed impressed. "Well, Amanda would certainly benefit from that. Would you like to go along, dear?"

"Sure!" Amanda grabbed her backpack and trotted right over to my car. She scooted into the backseat.

What? No! No! I wanted to shriek. Nothing against Amanda, but I didn't want her coming along. And I couldn't think of a quick way out. I leaned back against the headrest, disappointed.

"You don't mind, do you?" Marlene asked Maya. "There's just not a lot for her to do here with you gone."

"No problem," Maya said cheerfully. "So I guess we'll see you later. Probably not till four or so." She gave me an apologetic look as she climbed into the backseat.

Then Erin got back in the car and closed the door. I shifted the car into drive, and with a big wave for Marlene we were on our way.

"Thanks for saving me," Amanda said, settling in behind me. "My mother still thinks I'm safer with you guys than off with my friends. What a laugh."

Ha ha, I thought. *Big laugh*.

"I went through that stuff with my dad," Maya told Amanda. "I used to have to clear things two weeks in advance. No quick shopping trips or spontaneous runs for Chinese food."

"Which reminds me," Amanda said, popping her head between the two front seats. "Can you drop me at the mall?"

I glanced in the rearview mirror at Maya, who was shrugging. "No problem," I said, turning the corner.

"We will probably be gone for at least four

hours," Maya said. "Are you sure you can kill that much time at the mall?"

"Are you kidding? I've been dying to hang with my new boyfriend. He works in the ski shop, and I can chill in the back room and try to distract him." Amanda wrote something on a scrap of paper. "Here's my number. Call me on my cell when you get back into town and we'll hook up for inspection at the Castle."

I realized she'd picked up on our nickname for Maya's house. I pulled into the parking lot of the mall.

"Right here is good," Amanda said.

I stopped the car and let Amanda out.

"There goes trouble," Maya said as the fifteen-year-old strutted toward the mall without looking back.

"No, I think she's too smart to get in trouble," Erin commented. "More likely she'll get *you* in trouble one of these days."

I drove away from the mall and turned onto the highway. Erin rifled through the glove compartment and popped in an 'N Sync tape. Suddenly I felt a shot of adrenaline. This was it. We were on our way.

All morning I'd been trying not to think about the reality of it. I mean, in a few hours I'd be talking to my father. *Wait a minute*, I thought. *What if he's not home? Maybe I should have e-mailed that I was coming.* I decided it was better this way. A surprise. I know I said it was all about college money, but now I realized that Jessica might have been right. There was more to this. It had killed me to learn that my father was so close. Now, today, I was closing that distance between us.

Paper rattled beside me as Erin refolded a map. "I hope Dan gave us the right address," she said.

I hope . . . I hope . . . Gripping the steering wheel, I set my eyes on the flat horizon ahead. I could think later. Right now I needed to focus on getting us there.

As I drove, we talked about everything but my father and my college cash crisis. Erin e-mailed a hello to Matt from me on Maya's palm computer. Maya talked to Luke on her cell phone while Erin and I sang songs at the top of our lungs so that Maya couldn't hear him. Before I knew it Erin was directing me off the highway.

"Okay, the next light should be Woodmont, where you'll want to turn left," Erin said, looking up from the map.

I tried to focus only on Erin's directions, but I could no longer block out the feelings that swelled inside me. I was going to see my dad. I was nervous and excited and scared. It would be a miracle if I didn't burst into tears at the first sight of him.

"And . . . that's it up ahead," Erin said. "You want to turn right by that mailbox—that's Caswell Lane. From there he should be a block and a half away, on the left."

Caswell Lane. It was an ordinary suburban street with houses that looked very similar to each other. One with blue shutters, one Tudor style, next to another with a sparkling picture window in front. Nothing special about this block except that my dad probably drove down it a few times each day.

My heart beat faster as Erin pointed to the house on the left. I pulled my car to the curb and parked on the opposite side of the street. I was trying to ignore the painful lump in my throat. Why was I getting so emotional? It was just a house, right? And even if my dad walked right out this moment, what was the big deal?

There lives the man who walked out on his family seven years ago! I wanted to shout at myself. *Don't think he's going to get all choked up and misty-eyed about seeing you again!*

"That's it," Erin said. "I wonder if he's home."

"There's a car in the driveway," I noted. "Maybe it's his."

I turned off the engine, and the car fell silent as

we all stared at the gray house with the blue shutters. A picture window. A small garage. A wooden fence enclosed the side yard. An unremarkable house. Anybody could live there.

"What's that by the gate?" Maya asked.

I tilted my head and squinted. It was nearly hidden by the car, but I could see it now.

"It's a tricycle," Erin said.

A *pink tricycle*, I thought. Did we have the wrong house? Why would a little girl's bike be parked in my dad's driveway? My thoughts swirled around the meaning of it. And then I realized. "Oh, God!" I cried. "My dad has another kid."

Chapter 5

I swallowed hard. A tight pain stabbed my stomach. I'd never imagined my father having other kids. *When did he get remarried?* I wondered. *How many more secrets does he have?*

"Well, it's been a long time since you've seen him," Erin pointed out as if it made perfect sense for Dad to start a new family.

But I had always thought of Dad just the way he was when he left for Arizona. As unrealistic as it sounds, I'd imagined that time stood still for him.

Flashing back to that last time we were together, I could see him so clearly. He had stopped by to return my brother's Walkman, but I'd figured that was just an excuse to take me out for ice cream. His blond hair was combed off to the side. His blue eyes were full of understanding and little flashes of excitement. And his smile—he had one of those smiles that make other people relax. I even remember what he was wearing that day: jeans and an old baseball jacket. He slung his arm around me, and the leather sleeve felt cold against my cheek, but I didn't mind.

"Wow, kids. That would be really weird. I guess a lot of things have changed about him," Maya said.

Erin snorted. "Yeah, maybe he's fat and bald."

Wind whistled around the car, and I shivered. "That is *so* not possible," I insisted. But even as I said it, I knew it was a very real possibility.

God, how could I have been so naive? I wondered. He's got a whole new family. He replaced me with another daughter—a little girl he probably tucked in every night. No wonder Dad didn't want me to know where he was living. He didn't want me to show up at his doorstep and complicate his new life.

"So what's the plan?" Maya asked.

"Definitely ring the doorbell," Erin said, making me aware that my palms were sweating despite the cold outside. "We can't sit here all day."

"Sure we can," I said. "Detectives do it all the time." I was stalling. How could I admit that I was shaking too much to make it up that sidewalk? How could I explain that suddenly I had no idea what I was doing there?

"We *could* have the wrong house," Maya said.

"What if Dan gave you—"

I tuned her out as something moving beside the house caught my attention. The side door swung open, and someone bounded down the stairs. I gasped, feeling a shudder of recognition. My father. A little more filled out, a little gray . . . "That's him," I said, not sure if I wanted Dad to see me.

Erin leaned across the steering wheel and peered through my window. "Not so fat. And not bald. But he's leaving, Ker. You better go catch him."

I wanted to. Really. But at the moment I was frozen in my seat. Across Caswell Lane my father climbed into a green SUV. I stared as the car started. A puff of warm air came from the tailpipe.

"Yo, girlfriend." Erin snapped her fingers a few times. "Don't *make* me pull you out of that seat and take you over there."

Dad's car was backing out of the driveway. Erin yanked on the sleeve of my jacket. "He's leaving!" she cried.

"What should we do?" Maya asked. Erin reached over and turned my head toward the windshield. "Well, follow him, for starters," she said. "Turn key, press pedal, turn wheel."

I let out my breath, a little embarrassed that I was panicking. Then I started the car. I was doing it. Checking for traffic, I pulled onto the road a few yards behind my father's car.

"I have to call Luke back," Maya said, dialing her phone. "This is so exciting. Just like in the movies."

Not that he was hard to follow on a quiet street with a stop sign at nearly every intersection. "I don't know, Maya," I said. "A car chase through suburban Milwaukee is not exactly good material for the next *Mission Impossible* movie."

Maya flipped her phone shut. "He's not home anyway."

When Dad turned out of the development and onto a highway, I was right behind him. We passed a car dealership, a steak house, an elementary school. The school had a playground with colorful monkey bars and slides. My brain cataloged everything while my stomach churned. *You are entering dangerous territory! Turn back now! Painful emotions ahead,* I thought.

Like a fool, I drove on.

"How long are we going to follow him?" Maya asked.

"Hold on," I said. "I think he's pulling over."

The road curved to the left, then forked. Just beyond the fork, almost in the middle of the road, I spotted a gas station and a WAWA minimart. Dad turned in and pulled up to a pump.

I drove into the lot and braked. "He's getting

gas. Should we wait?"

"For what?" Erin asked. "His next oil change? Park the car and go talk to him."

I pulled the car into a spot and shut off the engine.

Maya's head popped forward between the seats. "Maybe she doesn't want to talk to him anymore," she told Erin. "Are you okay, Kerri?"

I nodded, realizing it was a total lie. But I wasn't about to admit to my friends how hurt I felt already, just knowing that Dad had another kid. I mean, that didn't change anything for me, right? I was still his daughter. He was still feeling guilty about leaving . . . right?

"So you go, girl," Erin said, nudging me toward the door.

Easy for you to say, I thought. My insides quivered as I forced myself to pull the handle, push the door, swing my legs out. *You can do this,* I told myself. *You're not here for an* Oprah *reunion. You're here for your college survival.*

I got out of the car and braced myself against the cold wind. Zipping my jacket, I waited as my friends climbed out. Maya gave me this look of awe, as if she didn't think I'd really do it.

"We'll go get some munchies and stuff," Erin said, pulling on Maya's sleeve.

Maya nodded. "Good luck, Ker."

I shoved my hands into my pockets and stepped toward my father. He was holding a gas nozzle, sort of leaning against the side of his car. His red squall jacket was zipped up to the top, his gray-blond hair curled over the high collar. Michael Hopkins. God, he looked like any stranger getting gas on a cold afternoon.

The wind was already making my eyes water. I swiped away the tears. I didn't want him to think I was crying over him. I marched up to him and paused. My breath caught in my throat when he glanced at me.

His blue eyes caught mine. A polite look at first. Then a flicker of something. Pain? Surprise? I wasn't sure.

I wasn't sure if he even knew who I was.

Chapter 6

"**K**erri? Is that you?" My father let go of the gas line and stepped toward me. "It's so . . . it's great to see you." He touched my shoulder. "What are the chances of this?"

My throat felt so tight. I swallowed hard, determined not to get emotional. "It wasn't an accident," I told him. "I drove here to find you."

"Really?" He seemed impressed. "I mean, when you stopped answering my e-mails . . . "

All my fear about seeing him suddenly turned to anger. Why was he acting so casual? Didn't he think it was a big deal to see his daughter after seven years? Didn't he care that I'd caught him in his lie about living in Arizona?

"Oh, don't talk to me about e-mails, Dad," I said. "I stopped answering them when I found out you moved back to Wisconsin without telling any of us. And I know that . . . that you have a wife and a kid. Or is it more than one kid? Or maybe you have another family in Arizona too. How many other lies do I need to find out about?"

He flinched. "Kerri, I . . ."

I waited. For what, I don't know. Searching for words, he stared off in the distance. As if the answers would appear on cue cards down by the car dealership.

"You're upset, and I don't blame you," he said. "Hell, I'd be mad at me too. I haven't been the best father to you over these years. I know that, and I'm sorry. But I didn't lie to you, honey. I never lied. If I neglected to tell you I was moving up here, it's—"

"It's the same thing," I said, feeling my voice rise. I'd gone through this scene in my head too many times over the years to let him turn things around. Not now. Not after seeing his nice little house with a yard for his kid to play in. A house with a yard, after my mom had to sell our house in Kensington Heights and take an apartment because she couldn't pay the mortgage. After she worked summers and gave up all kinds of things to feed and clothe my brother and me. No, I wasn't going to let this man get away with that. "Look, Dad, I didn't drive all the way up here to be your new best friend or anything," I told him. "Yes, I tracked you down, but I came to make you an offer."

He nodded, eyeing me curiously.

"I'm going to college in the fall," I said defiantly. "And I want you to help pay for it."

My father nodded again. Then he smiled. "Well, Kerri, that's some offer," he said, his eyes sparkling. "An irresistible offer. Sign me up."

I wasn't sure if he was joking to lighten things up or seriously agreeing to pay the money. "Are you making fun of me?" I asked.

"I'm not!" He held up his hands defensively. "I'm dead serious. There's nothing I'd like more than to pay for your college education. It—it would make me feel really good. I want to do it. Really."

I blinked, speechless.

"Sorry if I sounded flip before," he went on. "I'm just a little blown away by . . . by all of this. Guy runs out for gas and ends up face-to-face with his long-lost daughter on a freezing cold afternoon." He blew on his hands, then shoved them into his pockets. Then he fixed his eyes on me. Those smiling eyes. He used to be so full of fun and games. Now I wasn't sure how to read him.

"I guess it doesn't get this cold in Arizona," I said.

"Ouch!" he replied, making a joke of ducking. "I'd get into that with you, but by the time we reached the juicy stuff, we'd both be frozen stiff.

Why don't you come back to the house with me?
Sandy and Gabby would love to meet you. Sandy—
my wife—knows all about you and Dan. And to
answer your other question, no, there are no other
children. No other secret families. Just Gabby. She's
five. And she's going to run circles around you and
Dan if you give her a chance. She's a real handful,
but I think you'll like her."

I shook my head. *I can't believe you have
another daughter*, I wanted to say. *And you want me
to meet her? You want me to meet your new family,
the people who replaced me and Dan and Mom?* But
of course I didn't. "I have to go." I glanced over at
the WAWA. Maya and Erin were on their way out
the door, holding cups of coffee and what looked
like a box of doughnuts. They headed over to my
car. "My friends came with me, and they have to get
back," I lied.

"Hey, Kerri!" Erin called. "Throw me the keys
and I'll bring your car over to the pumps."

"I gotta go," I said, fumbling through my jacket
pockets for the keys.

"Sure. All right," he said, raking his hair back.
He nodded at my friends, a friendly nod, like he
was running for mayor or something. "I'll send you
an e-mail, and we can set things up."

I nodded. "Yeah." I'd come for money, and I'd

gotten it. That was all I wanted . . . right? "'Bye," I said and then I turned and walked over to my car, where my friends were waiting.

"What happened?" Maya asked. She motioned toward my dad's SUV. He was pulling away.

"I'll tell you guys everything," I said. "But first can I use your cell phone, Maya? I've got to make a call."

She pulled it out of her backpack. "It's all yours."

"Thanks." I took it and dialed my home number, hoping my mother wouldn't pick up. I needed to talk to Dan.

"Hello?" he answered.

"You are not going to believe this," I said. "But first, is Mom there? She doesn't know I went to Milwaukee."

"You're in Milwaukee?" I could hear the surprise in his voice.

"You're the one who gave me Dad's address!" I pointed out.

"But I didn't think you'd actually go through with it."

I smiled. "That shows how much you know about me. Erin and Maya are here with me. Is Mom there?"

"She's at her yoga class," Dan replied. "So, did

you see him? Was he home?"

"Saw him. Saw his house. Saw his daughter's bike. Why didn't you tell me he had another family?"

Silence. Then Dan said, "I didn't know."

"But you've been e-mailing him all this time." I glanced over at Erin and Maya, who were fumbling with the driver's-side door, which was stuck, and pretending not to listen to my conversation.

"I told you we didn't get into that stuff," Dan said. "I didn't want to get personal with him."

I could hear the annoyance in his voice. "Whoa. *Someone's* got issues." I wasn't sure I wanted to dig into Dan's feelings in front of my friends.

"Sure I'm pissed," Dan went on. "Aren't you? I mean, he acts like he can't do the father thing, then turns around and starts all over again somewhere else. And in the meantime we get ditched. How do you explain that?"

"I don't know," I said. "But he did agree to one thing. He's paying my college bills."

"Wow." It must have taken a minute for that to sink in. "What's his house like?" he asked.

I thought about the two-story house I'd stared at so intently. "Nice, but not that big a deal. It was just so weird seeing him and talking to him. And you know what? He recognized me. Even before I said anything, he knew it was me." Somehow that mattered to me a lot.

"Well, I'm glad I didn't have to see him to get *my* money," Dan said. But I wondered how much of Dan's cool attitude was just that—attitude.

Maya called Amanda to stage a rendezvous at the mall. I had given my friends the play-by-play of my talk with my father on the ride back to Madison. They were totally psyched that he agreed to help pay for college. When we pulled into the parking lot outside Nordstrom's, Amanda was standing by the doors with a tall guy whose head was shaved.

She kissed him good-bye and climbed into the backseat. "Hey, how'd it go?" she asked.

"Great," I said. "How about you?"

"Excellent." Amanda stretched out. "I spent the whole time with Kevin in the stockroom. His boss is really cool. Kevin wants me to try to get away from the sleepover tonight and meet him at the Cellar. I told him I'd try but I wasn't sure."

I could understand Amanda wanting to spend Saturday night with her boyfriend, but I couldn't see her sneaking out of the Castle without getting caught.

Amanda turned to Maya. "Do you know if Mom and Spencer are going out tonight?"

"Don't count on it," Maya said. "Not when I'm having friends over."

"Oh, well," Amanda said as we pulled up to the Castle. "Maybe next weekend."

As Amanda and Erin ran into the house to use the bathroom, Maya waited outside with me. While I grabbed my backpack from the trunk, she straightened up the car, stuffing half-empty cups and snack wrappers into a trash bag.

"You know," she said, "I don't mind Amanda, but Marlene is another story. She's always here. It's like my dad and I never have the house to ourselves anymore."

"I know." I could feel Maya's tension. Since her mother died, Maya's life has been one change after another. She was trying to be cool about it, but I wasn't sure she was ready to deal with this particular transition. It seemed that Marlene and Maya's dad were getting kind of serious.

Inside, we settled into Maya's room, which is big and comfortable, unlike the rest of the Castle, which is sort of big and uncomfortable. She's got a comforter and curtains covered with a tiny rosebud print—very sweet, like Maya. One wall is covered with cool built-in pine shelves filled with books, CDs, and Maya's treasured collection of antique dolls that her mom started for her.

Maya and Erin turned on some music and started sorting through the enormous CD collection. Amanda stretched out on Maya's fluffy four-poster bed to read the latest issue of **seventeen**. A few minutes later Jessica arrived. She kicked off her sneakers and pulled a bag of chips out of her backpack.

"I hope we're eating some real food tonight, because I didn't have time for lunch," she said, tearing open the bag of chips. "I spent the whole afternoon in the library on campus."

"Don't worry, we're having pizza," Maya said.

"Poor you," I told Jess, grabbing a chip. "I spent the whole afternoon finding my father."

Jessica crunched down on a mouthful of chips, then swallowed with a gulp. "You went through with it! How did it go? Tell me! Did you talk to him?"

I shook my head. "Been there, done that." I stretched out on the thick cream carpeting and told Jessica everything. She was appropriately blown away.

"Now all you need is a way to break it to your mom," she said. "She's going to be really upset to hear he's got a wife and another kid."

Erin glared at Jessica. "I don't see why she has to tell her mother at all." She tried on one of Maya's scarves and looked in the mirror. "He's your father, Kerri," she said. "It's your business."

Jessica sighed. "Liz is going to find out eventually."

"Yeah," Maya agreed. "But how do you break that kind of news to your mother?"

Jessica grinned. "Hey, I know. We could make it a secret, and *Erin* can blab it out." She stared at Erin. "You're pretty good at that, aren't you?"

"Get over it, Jessica!" Erin turned so fast, the scarf wafted to the ground.

"Come on, Erin. It was just a joke," Jessica said, blinking innocently. "When did you get so sensitive?"

Erin picked up the scarf and wound it through the air. "When did *you* become such a comedian?"

"Give it a rest, you guys," I said, sitting cross-legged on the floor. "I've got this huge thing to drop on my mom. And there will never be a good time to just blurt it out."

"Why don't you bake her a cake and write the message on the top?" Amanda leaned over to grab a handful of Jessica's chips. She started munching on them.

I smiled. "My mom's flaky, but not *that* flaky."

"You need to take Liz out to lunch—somewhere nice on State Street," Maya insisted.

"Woman to woman. She'll listen to you."

"You're probably right," I said, sighing. "But let's talk about something else now," I added. "We're supposed to be having fun, right?"

Erin threw back her scarf and clicked on Maya's television. "There's a beauty pageant on tonight," she said. "I don't know what time, but I've got to see it. It's so much fun trashing the outfits."

Just then there was a knock on the door, and Marlene peeked in. "Hey, girls. Why the closed door? Something secret going on in here?" She walked into the room.

Maya swung toward Marlene with a stack of CDs in her arms. "I always keep the door closed. The music disturbs Dad."

"He's playing pool now, so I don't think he minds." Marlene patted Amanda's leg.

Amanda dropped the magazine. "What?"

"Just wondering how you can concentrate on reading when the music is so loud. Anyway, it's time to come downstairs. We're going to make—" She paused to swoop down and pick up Jessica's potato chip bag from the floor. "Who's been eating this junk?"

And who invited the food police? I thought.

Amanda wiped her hands on her jeans. "Not me," she said quickly.

"I brought them," Jess answered. "I didn't get a chance to eat lunch."

"It's bad to skip meals," Marlene told Jessica. "See how overhungry you get? But we have some healthy snacks downstairs. I left the pizzas for you girls to assemble."

Jessica shrugged, but there was a definite tension in the air. Usually when we hung out at each other's homes, the parents left us alone. Now here was Marlene butting in. She wasn't even one of our moms. I could see how that would get on Maya's nerves.

"We'll be right down," Maya told her.

Erin tossed the scarf back into the bin but tied a fringed belt around her hair. "Yeah, baby," she said, taking a last look at herself in the mirror.

Everyone headed downstairs to the billiards room, where Mr. Greer, dressed in casual slacks and a button-down shirt, was setting up a game. "Hey, girls. Who wants to play?"

"I'm in," Erin said.

"I think I'll get the pizza going," Maya said.

"I'll help," I told her. Not that I didn't like pool, but I could tell that Maya had something on her mind.

"I'm up for a game," Jessica challenged. "We can play teams. I'll take Amanda."

"Let's have Amanda play on Spencer's team," Marlene insisted. "She needs some tutoring in the art of . . ."

Her voice faded as I followed Maya into the kitchen. She closed the swinging door behind her. "Is it my imagination or is that woman butting into everyone else's business?" she asked.

"Marlene? She's pushy, but I think she means well."

"I think she means to be the next Mrs. Greer," Maya said, taking ingredients out of the industrial-size refrigerator. She placed them on the Formica island in the center of the kitchen. "She's already acting like she lives here. I just hate the way she has to be in charge of everything. Leave this open, don't eat that, do it this way."

"She's definitely bossy," I said. "But your dad seems to like her."

"Yeah. Too bad." Maya handed me a glob of dough and started pressing another mound into a flat circle. "Dad goes out of his way to make Marlene feel at home. I know he likes her, and I mean, I'm okay about him dating and everything. But this thing with Marlene is freaky. It's like she's jumping into my mother's shoes. Literally. I wouldn't be surprised to find her rooting through Mom's closet."

I looked up from the pizza dough. Tears sparkled in Maya's eyes.

"Okay, not really," Maya continued. "But the woman is *not* my mother." She swiped at her face with the sleeve of her shirt, then reached for the tomato sauce. "She's just not."

The kitchen was quiet except for a sniffle from Maya. I wondered how Maya must feel with those strangers in her house all the time. Strangers who might turn out to be her next family.

"You know," I said, popping a piece of grated cheese into my mouth, "no one will ever replace her. She'll always be your mom. Marlene can't take that away."

Maya nodded and sniffled again.

Somehow I wasn't sure I was helping. Family stuff wasn't exactly my area of expertise. In fact, I could use a few tips myself. Just that day I discovered another branch of my own family: a stepmother and a little sister. And here Maya had been going through this family merge thing for months. Who was I to give advice?

"It's so weird," I said. "Adopt a stepmother. Act like this one's your sister. Wake up one morning and you have an instant family. I have to say, I freaked when my father invited me to meet his wife and kid." I shook my head. "They're total strangers.

What happens if I don't like them and don't want to be part of their family? How do I make it work?"

"I've been thinking about stuff like that too." Maya bit her lip. "I don't have the answers," she said. "Just lots of questions."

I sighed and started slicing mushrooms for the pizza. "Me too," I told her. "Me too."

Chapter 7

"**H**ello up there!" Matt called from behind me on the path. "Why are you running so fast? Is someone giving out free hot chocolate on State Street?"

"Got to . . . stay . . . warm," I panted, running in place so that he could catch up. It was Sunday morning, and we were jogging on our favorite path around Lake Mendota, but it was cold. Really cold. The wind made my eyes tear, which I'm sure turned to little ice crystals in my lashes.

"Okay, here's another question," Matt said as we continued down the path. "Did you decide what's next for you and your dad? I mean, do you think you'll go up there to meet his new family?"

"I don't know," I said honestly. Last night at Maya's, after everyone was asleep, I called Matt to tell him about the road trip. His question kept me awake almost all night. "Part of me wants to get to know them. But the thought of meeting strangers who are supposed to become my family . . . I think I'd rather get my teeth drilled by the dentist. Or sit through a really bad student production of *Macbeth*."

"Nervous is good," Matt replied. "But don't let that stop you from getting to know your dad. Your trip yesterday was a huge deal. You opened the door to a lot of possibilities. It looks like you and Dan have a shot at getting to know your father again."

"Not Dan," I said. "He's not interested. Or at least that's what he says." I ran silently, thinking about Dan and how he insisted he wanted nothing to do with Dad. It was definitely a cover for other feelings, but that was the way Dan operated. King of denial. It wasn't as if I could do anything about that.

"One more question," Matt said. His breath was a white stream of air as he jogged beside me. "Why are we the only idiots running out here? It's got to be thirty below out here."

I laughed. "You tell me. You're the one who suggested it. I figured you wanted to stay in shape for football."

"Football. . . . You sound like my parents. The season's over, but they've already got the schedule for next year's games at Purdue. Can you believe that?"

"Matt." I stopped running. Matt stopped too.

"You've got to talk to your parents about Boston College. You've got to tell them that's where you want to go."

"I know," Matt agreed. "I wanted to say something yesterday, but then I saw that football schedule. They really want me to go to Purdue. Family tradition or something. It's like I'm letting them down if I don't." He sighed. "I don't know how to break it to them. I'll probably end up going there just to make them happy."

I didn't know what to say to make Matt feel better. All I could do was be there for him. I stood on my toes and wrapped my arms around his neck and hugged him.

"All this college stuff," he murmured, squeezing back. "It's so much pressure. Between my parents and us going to different schools, it's a lot to think about."

"I know," I said, wishing desperately that I could help him. And then an idea popped into my head. A plan. An awesome plan. One that would totally cheer up my boyfriend. And I was going to start it today.

"This is going to be so cool," Jessica said that afternoon. Mom was off at her Sunday afternoon feng shui class. Jess had agreed to come over and help me out with my plan to cheer up Matt. She sat cross-legged on my daybed, flipping through the tan leather date book I had bought at the stationery store.

I'd already filled in a few dates, like my birthday and Matt's. I drew floating hearts all around Valentine's Day.

"You already downloaded Purdue's calendar for the fall semester," Jessica said. "I can't believe they plan that far ahead. So he's definitely going there, then?"

"It looks that way, even though that's not his first choice." I sorted through the pages I'd printed. "Let's see. I've got the basics. The day school starts. Holidays. Football schedule. We can take turns flying out to see each other every other weekend or so."

"Is there an airport near Purdue?" Jessica asked. "What town is it in again?"

"Fort Wayne, Indiana," I said, clicking onto a travel website. "Let's me try a flight directly there and see what comes up." I typed in the information for a round-trip fare from Miami. A few seconds later the whole list of flights and airlines popped onto the screen.

"Yes!" I said. "I can fly directly there. A hundred and ninety-eight bucks."

"Ouch!" Jessica said. "You guys are going to

have to come up with some substantial commuting cash."

"Yeah," I admitted. "But I'm sure we'll both have jobs on campus. And we'll take turns flying. Or maybe I can con some people into doing a road trip up there sometime. So now I just need to figure out which weekends are important to be together." I sifted through the printout of Purdue's football schedule. "Here's Purdue's homecoming on October fourteenth. I can fly to Indiana for Matt's homecoming game, and he can come to Miami for mine."

"Unless they're on the same weekend," Jessica pointed out.

"They can't be . . . they won't be," I insisted, turning back to the computer. I clicked onto the University of Miami website. "No, Miami's homecoming isn't until November. Whew!" I pretended to wipe sweat from my forehead, then printed the Miami calendar.

"Okay, you lucked out with homecoming," Jessica said, making a note on the legal pad we were scribbling on. "What about spring break? That's a biggie."

"I'll figure it out as soon as Miami's schedule finishes printing." I swung my chair away from the screen and smiled at my friend. "Thanks for helping me with this. This is just what Matt needs. Maybe if he can leaf through the date book and see how the actual days and weeks play out, he'll feel better about us going to different colleges. Maybe it will cheer him up about going to Purdue also."

Jessica nodded. "It's a great idea. If I still had Alex as a boyfriend, I'd do the same thing."

"Alex? I thought you were getting over him," I said, feeling bad for her.

"I am." Jessica frowned. "I don't know. Maybe I'm just feeling sorry for myself that I don't have a boyfriend. Someone to make plans with."

Before I could respond, the e-mail icon binged. I twirled back toward the computer. "It's from my dad," I said.

"You sound surprised," Jessica said. "The guy did say he was going to e-mail you."

"I guess in the back of my head I didn't want to get my hopes up. You know, just in case he didn't come through." I bit my lip. "And Dan's been so negative about the whole thing, which is weird since he's the one who suggested I hit up Dad for the money in the first place."

"Typical brother," Jessica said.

I nodded. "And it doesn't help that I can't talk to my mom about it. I still haven't found a way to break it to her that my dad has a new family."

"That's not an easy one," Jessica said, pushing her long dark hair back and stretching.

"Tell me about it," I said. Then I called to my brother across the hall. "Hey, Dan! Check this out."

"Yeah?" he muttered from the shadows of his room. By the time he'd come into my room, I'd skimmed Dad's e-mail.

Leaning over my shoulder, Dan read aloud: "Hope you can visit soon and meet everyone here. Gabby is thrilled to have a big sister, and Sandy looks forward to meeting you." He whistled through his teeth. "Sounds like domestic bliss to me. You going to meet the new fam?"

I shrugged. "Maybe. Or maybe I'll just give him our address and let him send the checks here," I said, testing him with the most callous answer I could think of.

Dan stepped away from my PC and folded his arms over his gray sweatshirt. "You're weird."

I frowned. "That's coming from an expert on weirdness."

Jessica leaned back on my cream-colored bedspread and pretended to leaf through a magazine. She'd watched Dan and me argue before and usually stayed out of it.

Not that Dan seemed to care. He rubbed a hand over his bristly head. "You just want the money. Isn't that a little cold?"

"Hello?" I couldn't believe him. "One minute you're pissed at Dad for having a nice house and a new family while we're living in this apartment. Now you're calling me greedy because I want a college education? I don't think so."

"It's not about college, Kerri," he said. "It's about playing daddy's little girl just to get his money."

"Isn't that what *you* did?" I asked him. "You took money for your business and didn't even try to see him. Oh, but that's okay, and I'm a brat?"

Dan shook his head, acting like I was the stupidest thing to come down the pike since Beanie Babies. "Fine. Let him save you." He walked out.

"What's that supposed to mean?" I called after him. He wasn't making any sense. Why should he be angry with me for getting money from Dad? He did the same thing!

No answer—just a slamming door and then a blast of rock music from his room.

Jessica sat up and turned toward Dan's door. "Is that your final answer?" she called.

I smiled at Jessica as she fell back onto the bed, grinning. "Can you believe he's trying to make me feel guilty?" I asked, swiveling back and forth in the computer chair.

Jessica waved her hand at Dan's door. "What did I say? Brothers. Can't live with them, can't kill them."

I appreciated her joke, but Dan's point was still bugging me. What was wrong with letting my father save me from a lifetime in this room, attending community college, while everyone else I knew flew off to cool, exciting places? If Dad could save me from a lifetime of Danhood, why shouldn't I let him be my hero? "Am I wrong?" I asked Jessica. "Is it wrong to take money from my father so that I can go to college?"

"Definitely not," Jessica replied. "Everyone knows you've totally flipped for the University of Miami. When something is that important, you have to go for it."

"Right," I said.

"Well, on that note." Jessica stood up and hoisted her backpack onto one shoulder. "I have another meeting on campus tomorrow. More research. Blah-blah-blah." Jessica was enrolled in a special program that allowed her to get a head start on college. Some afternoons she left high school early and attended classes at the University of Wisconsin.

"Thanks again for your help," I said, walking her to the door. "Be careful driving home. It's starting to snow."

"I'll be fine." She opened the door. "E-mail me when you finish the date book. Matt's going to love it."

"Later," I said, watching her walk down the corridor to the stairs. I couldn't help thinking about how I once lived down the block from Jessica. It was years ago, when my parents were still together and we were all living at the house in Kensington Heights.

I went back into my room, sat at the computer, and stared at Dad's e-mail. Back then he was so accessible. He was my hero all the time, saving me from awful, terrible fates at least once a day.

I remembered one shopping trip. I couldn't have been more than six. Mom sent us out for milk or soap or something. Of course, the grocery store was in a shopping center with an ice cream parlor and a drug store. I started pointing out things that I wanted, and Dad rushed to fulfill my every wish. A light-up necklace. An ice-cream cone. A purple pony with a beautiful rainbow-colored mane. Dad never could say no. That is, until he left. Then he didn't say anything.

And now here he was. He wanted to give me money for school. He wanted me in his life again. Wanted me to meet his family. His *new* family. I wasn't sure if I was ready for that.

I clicked Respond and thought about what I wanted to write. *Keep it light*, I told myself, and banged out the e-mail to my father.

> **Padre—**
> I'll bet you were shocked to see me at that WAWA yesterday. But you know I always liked surprises. Anyway, I'd love to meet everyone, but things are crazy right now. Senior year. Major study crunch before senioritis can set in.
> Which reminds me—college. I got a green light for early admissions from the University of Miami, my destiny. It's a rocking school, especially for my major (physical therapy). Must have room deposit—that's $1500—by next Thursday. Ten days!

I tried to picture Dad with his new daughter. Was he out there buying her ice cream and toys? Did she look like me at all? Would people be able to guess that we were sisters? Well half-sisters, but who's counting? I realized that I really did want to meet her. I wasn't the cold, calculating money-grubber Dan made me out to be. I stormed across the hall to tell my brother that.

The music filled the hall. He'd never hear me knocking. I turned the knob, but the door was locked. "Dan!" I shouted, banging on the door. "Dan! Open up!"

No answer. I wasn't sure if he didn't hear me or didn't *want* to hear me. That sort of summed up my relationship with Dan. He was there for me, whenever he was in the mood.

I went into the living room, which was also vibrating from the music. Mom was still at her class. Any minute one of our neighbors would be banging on the door, complaining about the music. And who would have to answer? Not Dan. Not Mom. Me.

It wasn't fair. I plopped down on the sofa and sandwiched two pillows over my ears. At the moment a family merge had new appeal. Maybe having a new sister wouldn't be such a bad thing after all.

Chapter 8

Monday morning I didn't even care that the sky was steely gray and that cold, icy slush had oozed through my shoes as I walked across the parking lot of South Central High School. As I climbed the front steps and passed through the double doors of the building, I realized how much had changed since I'd walked past the exact spot just last Friday night.

I'd reconnected with my father. I'd found a way to pay the bills at the University of Miami. And I'd come up with a killer schedule that would keep Matt and me together through our first year of college. I smiled to myself as I headed upstairs to my locker. *Not bad for one weekend,* I thought.

"You're looking up today," Matt said as I plucked him away from a circle of guys hanging out by a bulletin board. He walked backward so that he could study me. "What happened? Are all tests canceled due to lack of interest?"

I grinned. "Something even better."

"*School* is canceled?" He grabbed my hand and yanked me toward the doors at the end of the corridor. "That's perfect. If we leave now, we can make it to the ski slopes before lunch."

"Come on," I said, yanking him back, nearly knocking into a boy carrying a huge poster. As I swung out of the kid's way, my backpack slipped off my shoulder and crashed onto the floor.

"Oops." I'd left the zipper open, and stuff came spilling out. A tube of lip gloss rolled across the floor, my keys jangled onto the tile, and the new date book I'd bought for Matt slipped out.

"Double darn," I said, lunging for the slender book.

"You curse like a Saturday-morning cartoon character." Matt snatched the book and held it up. Somehow, he realized I didn't want him to notice it. "What's this?"

The gift was wrapped in a satin ribbon. A tiny silk rose was tied into the delicate bow.

"It's just . . . something," I muttered, swiping at it.

But Matt held it out of my reach. "*Something?* Points off for lack of description. 'Something' is not a word on Mr. Yolanski's vocabulary list."

I sighed, putting the stuff on the floor back in

my pack. "Well, it was supposed to be a surprise—for later—but I guess now is good too." I pointed to the date book. "It's for you," I said. "But I guess you already figured that out."

"You got me a date book?" he asked, eyeing the gift.

"Look inside. It's filled in—at least for next fall."

He untied the ribbon, seeming a little confused. This wasn't going the way I'd planned. He wasn't getting it.

"I guess I should explain," I added. "I know you've been a little worried about us being so far apart. So when I found out that Dad would pay my room and board at the University of Miami, I started planning stuff for us. For almost every weekend, starting from the day I have to fly down to Miami in September."

Matt's eyes flashed up at me. But it wasn't the happy expression I had expected. He didn't seem exactly thrilled.

"I did it for you," I told him. "I went online and downloaded the calendars from the University of Miami and Purdue. I compared their schedules, then I—"

"Wait." He shook his head. "Who says I'm going to Purdue? I haven't even heard about the scholarship or—"

"But yesterday you said you were going there, and you know you'll get in," I reassured him. "You're a great student, and those football scouts were so impressed by you. They came to three different games."

"It's just . . ." He stood there, bending the book in his hands.

Silence. This definitely wasn't good. Why wasn't Matt as excited about our plans as I was?

"Let me just show you what I did," I said, gently taking the book. I opened it to September, where I'd put a little airplane sticker on the date I had to depart for Florida. "See? This is the day I leave for school. And here's the weekend you'll probably leave. But I figure I'll drive to Purdue with you. Maybe bring the car back for your parents? Since you start before I do, I can help you settle in."

I glanced up at him. None of this seemed to be registering.

"Anyway, I marked important dates, like homecoming at both schools—things we won't want to miss. I figure I'll fly to Purdue for yours, and you can come to Miami for mine." I handed him the date book. "And I found a few websites that help you get really cheap air fares. We might have to change planes, but it's no big deal flying from Miami to Fort Wayne. And we have plenty of time to make flight reservations and things like that."

He shook his head. "Flights . . . every other week? That'll cost us a bundle."

"Well . . . I know," I said. "But I figure we'll rack up enough frequent-flier miles to get a few free trips." I glanced at Matt. I wanted him to love my plan. I wanted him to jump in and go crazy planning the way I did over the weekend. "Oh, Matt," I said, trying not to let disappointment seep into my voice. I reached for his hand and squeezed it tight. "This is going to be great. Really! Don't you love my plan? Tell me you love it."

"It's . . . it's so you," he admitted, staring at the date book. He smiled reluctantly. "It's quintessential Kerri. I've got a plan, here I go!"

That was me all right. Only at the moment Matt didn't seem to like the quintessential me. I felt a knot forming in my throat. "What's wrong?" I asked.

"It's just . . . I don't know." He took the date book, closed it, and handed it back to me.

The knot in my throat grew heavier. "It's just a plan. Something to look forward to."

"But that's not how we do things," he said. "It's like, you feel like going to a movie? Yeah, sure, and we go. This . . ." His eyes darkened, and he shrugged. "It's too much. Kind of pushy."

"I don't get it," I said as my heart sank. "You

said that you were going to miss me. You said that being apart was going to be too hard." I searched his eyes, trying to find the reason he was acting so differently. "What do you want?"

Matt stared back at me. He opened his mouth as if to say something but then closed it again.

"What?" I pressed.

"Uhhh . . . a pretzel?" he joked. "That sounds good."

I felt too sick to laugh. Too sick to look him in the eye anymore.

"No. I'm serious," he said, grabbing my hand. "I'm starving. We have time to catch the pretzel guy before homeroom."

"Well, at least you're clear on that," I said.

"When it's time to eat, I am *always* very decisive," Matt said with a grin.

I tried to come up with a funny reply, but all I could do was wonder why Matt didn't like my plan. What was he really thinking?

I let myself meet his eyes again. His old smile was back. And I felt a sliver of hope that things weren't as bad as they seemed. We were still okay, Matt and I. At least for now.

But what about after that? I wondered. *What about next year?*

Chapter 9

"Who can figure out guys?" I asked as Erin applied glittery polish to my nails. It was four days later. Friday after school, my house. We were supposed to be doing homework together, but we decided to give each other manicures instead. "Matt gets all upset that we're going to be miles apart next year. I put together this calendar to show him that it doesn't have to be that way, and he gets all freaky."

"Something must have set him off." Erin sat cross-legged on my cream-colored quilt. She stuck the cap on the bottle and shook it vigorously. "Maybe he was having a bad day. How has he been acting since then?"

"Totally normal," I said. "It's been almost four days, and I haven't heard a word about college or the date book." I shook my head. "I just don't get him."

"Well, if you guys are going to the movies with

Luke and Maya tonight and then to the winter festival tomorrow, I'd say things are pretty okay."

"I guess," I said. "But I wish I could talk to him about this."

"Communication . . ." Erin sighed. "One of the elusive mysteries of life." She dabbed at my pinkie nail, than capped the bottle of polish. "All set to dazzle."

"Thanks." I lifted my hands and blew on fingernails covered with pale blue lacquer and silver glitter. "Are you sure you don't want to come with us tonight?" I asked her. "You know Maya and Luke would be cool with it."

"No, that's okay." Erin reached down to grab her backpack off the floor.

"Come on, Erin," I pressed her. "Ask Glen to come if you feel weird about being the only single one."

Erin slipped the bottles of polish inside her bag. "Glen's going out with that Tiffany girl tonight. Besides, I told Mr. Calvert I'd be at rehearsal. I want to measure the actors for costumes." She got up from the bed and paced the room. "Can you believe the costume girl quit the show?" she added. "Something about taking too much time, grades slipping, or whatever. The theater department is so lucky that I'm multitalented. Backdrops . . .

costumes . . ." She struck a glamorous pose. "I do it all, dahhhhling."

"You sure do," I said with a laugh. I crossed the room and sat at my computer to log on to the Internet.

Erin picked up a college catalog from beside my PC. "What's this?"

"More catalogs that my mom brought home. You know. Safety school. Get those applications out. Yadda, yadda. Something about me being a Virgo and not being compatible with Miami."

"Give me a break!" Erin cried. "Do you know my mom bought me this dull navy blazer for college interviews? As if I'd go within a hundred miles of a school that expects students to wear button-down shirts and blazers. Sometimes parents don't have a clue."

"At least my father didn't try to talk me out of going to Miami," I said, staring at my nails. I let my eyes go fuzzy for a minute. "I just wish he'd send the check for that deposit already."

"Is that why you were combing through the mail on the kitchen table earlier?"

"Am I that obvious?" I asked. So far no one but Matt knew about my latest after-school ritual: head home and paw through the mail for Dad's check.

"Yeah." Erin sat down on my bed with an

armful of catalogs. "I could tell something was up."

My computer connected to the server, but my mailbox was empty. "No mail," I said. I took a deep breath. "Okay, the truth is I'm getting nervous. I e-mailed Dad that I needed the deposit last Sunday. Five days ago. Since then I've been rushing home to intercept the mail and hide it from Mom. She still doesn't know I went to Milwaukee."

"The plot thickens," Erin said.

"I know I should tell her." I flopped back on the bed, keeping my nails in the air. "But I hate to see her get hurt. I hate to be the one hurting her."

Just then the e-mail binged on my computer. I went over and clicked it open. "What timing. It's from my dad."

> Hey, kiddo!
> I know you're busy, but school isn't seven days a week! Why don't you drive up this weekend? Sandy and Gabby just won't stop asking about you until they've met you. Plan to visit soon!
> Love, Dad

"Okay," Erin said, reading over my shoulder. "Sounds good to me. He really wants to see you."

"But no mention of the money." I bit my lip. "I

hate to sound so mercenary, but how can he be all 'let's be happy and get together' when he knows I'm here freaking out about this deadline?"

"Maybe he doesn't realize how much the money is freaking you out," Erin said. She sat back on the bed. Her raspberry-streaked pigtails went crooked as she tilted her head. "Are you going to visit him? You know, start a new relationship?"

I paused to think about it. "Yes," I said. I looked at her. "I think I want to give him a chance to be my father again." I glanced back at his e-mail. "But I can't go up there this weekend."

"Winter festival," Erin said knowingly.

I nodded, thinking of all the events: the sled races and the ice-sculpting and skating contests. "This is our last year to do it together." Staring at the screen of the computer, I frowned. "So what's a nice way to say, 'Sorry I can't make it, but where's the check?'"

Erin laughed. Then I heard another voice that made me panic.

"This is the answer to all our problems!" my mother was saying as she entered the doorway. She came into my room holding up a string from which a crystal the size of an almond was dangling.

Just the sight of her made me feel guilty. I grabbed on to the computer desk, glaring at the note on the screen. The words "Love, Dad" seemed to glow brighter than anything else. My heart started pounding. Would she see it? Should I try to change the screen really fast?

"Oh, hi, Erin," Mom said, waving the crystal at her. "How's everything?"

"Fine, Liz," Erin said. My mother tells all my friends to call her Liz. "So you're into feng shui now?"

"Just dabbling. But Lorraine Braden is becoming quite the expert," Mom went on, squeezing past me to the window. "People are actually paying her to feng shui their houses. Anyway, she says that with the way your room is set up, all the energy is flying right out the window. So a crystal should counteract that." She hung the clear string over the window latch.

I used the opportunity to get Dad's message off the computer screen.

"Just be careful in the spring when you open the window," Mom finished. She turned back to me, pushing up the sleeves of her sweatshirt. "What's wrong, Kerri?"

I hate how mothers have that sixth sense. I was tempted to say, "Nothing," and just let it go, but eventually I'd have to tell Mom about Dad. I braced myself, feeling tension seep into my shoulders.

"You're going to be mad, but I have to tell you," I admitted, feeling my face grow warm. "I went up to Milwaukee with Erin and Maya last weekend, and we found Dad."

Her eyes opened a little wider. "Really?"

"Um, I'd better get going." Erin stood up and grabbed her backpack. "You know how my parents get when I'm late for dinner."

"Okay," I said, understanding why she wanted to bail. "Thanks for the manicure. I'll see you tomorrow."

Erin ducked into the hall and gave me a thumbs-up that made me feel a little better. At least I had her support.

"Anyway, we went up to Milwaukee, and—"

"I knew it would happen sooner or later," my mother said, sighing. "Once you found out he was living so close by. But honey, you really should have told me you wanted to visit him. I wouldn't have been angry. Really."

"I know, Mom. I'm sorry. But—"

"It must have been an emotional experience for you, seeing your father after all these years," she added, sitting on my bed. "Are you okay?"

I nodded, a little surprised at how well she was taking the news. And it was funny how she could zero in on my feelings without having even been there. Sometimes my mother is so in tune with things. Other times I swear she lives in an alternate dimension. "It was strange seeing his house and everything. But the thing is . . ." I paused, trying to figure out a way to break the news about my father's other family. "One of the really surprising things . . . Oh, Mom, how can I say it in a way that won't hurt you?"

Mom blinked, concern in her eyes. "What is it, honey?"

I just had to say it. "Dad got married again. And they have a kid. A little girl. That part was weird, finding out about her. I—I'm sure it's upsetting for you too, but—"

"No," Mom said firmly. "Okay, I'm a little surprised, but I'm not upset about it. We've both defined new spaces. I moved on a long time ago."

"Really?" I asked. "I mean, doesn't it bother you that he has a new wife?"

She shook her head no. "Actually, I wish her luck. She's certainly going to need it," she said. "But you could have told me this last week."

Well, yeah, I thought, feeling the tension drain from my shoulders. I was glad to finally be open about it. But I couldn't believe that my mom was so laid back about this. She didn't seem hurt at all that Dad had moved on. *Is she hiding her pain from me?*

I wondered. *I can't tell.*

"So let's talk about you seeing your father," Mom continued. "That's a big deal, Kerri. What made you decide to go now? Curiosity?"

"More like desperation," I admitted. "You know how much I want to go to Miami. And we don't have the money, so I sort of cornered Dad, and the good news is that he's paying for my college room and board. Can you believe it?" I asked, smiling.

"I see," my mother replied. That was it. She didn't sound very enthusiastic. In fact, I noticed that Mom seemed almost tense. Very unlike her, since she began practicing Buddhism. Maybe she wasn't as laid back about my seeing Dad as I thought.

"Well, at least Miami is going to work out," I said. "So I don't have to worry about applying to other colleges."

"Look . . . Kerri, I don't want you to get your hopes up about this money," Mom began. "Believe me. In the end he'll only disappoint you. I think you should still fill out a few applications."

"Why are you saying this?" I found myself getting a little angry. "Things are finally working out. I'm going to Miami, and Dad's going to help me. Why can't you just be happy for me, Mom?"

"Because I know your father," she said, getting off the bed. "I know how he is with money. Remember the time your dad bought you a pony? He had to bring it back because he didn't think about how much it costs to feed and stable an animal."

I remembered. I was devastated when I had to give Carmel away. But that wasn't the point. "What does a horse have to do with college?" I asked, raising my voice.

My mother took a cleansing breath and moved a step toward me. "What I'm trying to tell you is that your father doesn't think ahead when it comes to money," she said in a quiet voice that made me even angrier. "He's made a lot of big promises in his lifetime, but he's never come through."

"But that was a long time ago," I said quickly. "People change." I wanted to believe that more than anything. Especially since Dad hadn't exactly come through for me yet. "And there's something else," I added. "Dad gave Dan five hundred dollars for his business. That proves that he's different now, doesn't it?" *It does*, I decided.

"He gave Dan money?" My mother raised her eyebrows. The surprise in her voice gave me a sense of triumph. "When?" she asked.

"I'm not sure," I told her. "But if Dad gave Dan

the money he needed, he'll give me the money I need."

"I don't know about that." Mom shook her head. "Five hundred dollars is a short-term commitment. That's something your father's good at. We're talking four years of room and board payments. And your dad's always had trouble with finances."

No, I thought, slumping into my computer chair. I didn't want Mom to be right. But the truth was that I had doubts about my father. *He hasn't exactly been Mr. Reliability in my life so far*, I thought. *And I haven't gotten a check yet. And he knows that I have a deadline.* No. I didn't want to think that way. Mom hadn't seen Dad in ten years. He could have become a totally different person, like, reformed or something.

I rested my head in my hands and stared at the mauve rug in the center of my room. All I knew was that my father had to keep his promise. Otherwise I didn't know what I would do.

Mom knelt down beside me and raised my chin with her hand. She gazed into my eyes. "Just promise me that you'll apply to at least one other college, okay?"

I looked away. "Yeah. Okay. Sure."

"That's all I'm asking," Mom said, then got up

to leave. She stopped at the door and turned. "Kerri, I hope I'm wrong about everything. I hope he really does come through for you. I just want you to be prepared if he doesn't, that's all."

"I know, Mom," I said, hoping that she was wrong about everything too.

As soon as she left my room, I worked on an e-mail to my father. Maybe if I reminded him about the deadline again, he'd realize how important this money was to me.

> **Sorry, but I can't make it this weekend. Big winter festival on Saturday—ice, snow, sledding. Maybe another weekend?**
>
> **And don't forget about that room deposit due next week (postmarked by Thursday). Please drop me an e-mail to let me know when you're sending it.**
>
> **Thanks for the help, Dad. I really appreciate it!**

I was reading over the e-mail when Matt appeared in the doorway.

"Hey, you," he said, leaning against the door frame. "Ready to head out?"

"Come, read this before I send it," I said, pointing to monitor. I showed him Dad's message, the one I was responding to. "Do you think it's too . . . pushy? Too much?" I nervously watched Matt read the screen. Wasn't that what he said about me a few days ago? That I was pushy? The thought of that awkward conversation still made me queasy.

He put his hands on my shoulders and massaged gently. "No, it's cool," he said, making me melt under his touch. "So you finally heard from him."

"Sort of," I said, clicking Send. "Let's just see how he answers this e-mail. I mean, the waiting is driving me crazy. Why doesn't he just send me the check or wire me the money? What if this isn't going to happen?"

"A lot of people can't come up with that kind of money on such short notice. I know my parents pay everything in installments. He might have to move some investments around."

I put my head down on the computer desk as Matt continued to rub my shoulders. "It's not just the money. It's the fact that he lied to me about living in Arizona. How am I supposed to totally believe him now? My mother says I should be prepared to be disappointed."

"Why don't you call the university?" Matt suggested. "Maybe the deadline isn't a big deal. Maybe you can get an extension. You know, just in case."

I lifted my head from the desk. "That's a great—"

BING! An e-mail message came in for me.

"I'm going to call Miami first thing tomorrow," I told Matt as I clicked on the message. It was from Dad. "He must be online right now." I opened the message.

Can feel your tension about the $$$. Not to worry. Will send the check out tomorrow.

Love, Dad

"Can you believe it?" I said, amazed. I was feeling better already. It was so easy for me to think the worst of my father. But it looked like he really was going to send me the money!

"Great news," Matt said after he'd read the message. "And you doubted him."

"Not anymore," I said, and I meant it. If I was going to accept money from my father, maybe I had to start trusting him. Maybe it was time to give the guy a little credit.

Chapter 10

"**G**o, Matt! You go!" I cried at the winter festival the next day. Sun glittered over the new layer of snow that had fallen last night. I held on to the sled and willed Matt to pull me faster across the frozen Lake Mendota. "Go!" I yelled again. "We can win this race!"

Hundreds of people stood on the sidelines, clapping and cheering on the competitors. Matt and I were nearing the finish, but Maya and Luke were in front of us. "One more pull and—" My voice caught as the sled flew over a hard bump. "You can do it!" I cried.

Matt trudged on, but Maya and Luke were too far ahead. As I urged our sled forward, Maya and Luke sailed across the finish line amid a burst of applause.

Matt and I slid across in second place. Not too shabby, and I could afford to be magnanimous since one of my best friends had come in first. Jessica and Erin were nowhere near the finish line. When I glanced back, they stood in the middle of their lane, trying to get the sled back on its runners. It looked like they'd had a spill and were arguing about it.

I sighed as Matt parked the sled safely on a mound of snow. "We tried," I said.

Matt collapsed onto the snow, flinging his arms out. "You were right. Next time you pull!"

I slid off the sled and rolled onto the snow beside him. My hat came off, exposing my messy hair, but I didn't care. "You were great," I told Matt. "I just like to direct things."

"Back sled driver," Matt teased, tucking a strand of hair behind my ear.

I laughed, feeling much closer to him than I had in days. Matt leaned close, gently touching his warm lips to mine.

"Kerri! Kerri!" someone called. It was a man's voice.

I sat up in the snow. "Who's that? Who's calling me?" My eyes scanned the white horizon under the wide-open blue sky.

Matt sat up beside me and looked around. He pointed toward one of the blue-and-yellow-striped tents set up on the terrace that bordered the lake.

The University of Wisconsin campus loomed behind them. "That man down there by the food tents, waving like crazy."

I followed his gaze until I spotted the guy. "I don't believe it," I murmured. "What's my father doing here?"

I watched him bound down the hill like an Olympic runner. *He read my e-mail*, I realized. *He came to deliver my check in person.*

Dad wasn't even out of breath when he ran up to Matt and me. "Hey, how's it going?" he asked, as if he stopped by every weekend to see how I was doing.

"I can't believe you're here," I told my father. "How did you find me?"

"You told me about the festival, and Dan gave me the details." Dad turned to Matt and put his hand out. "I'm Kerri's father, Michael Hopkins."

"Matt Fowler," he answered with a good hard shake. "It's good to meet you."

I could see my friends watching from their sleds. Erin started walking toward us. I was beginning to feel a little uncomfortable. I mean, after seven years, here was my father standing right in front of me, meeting my boyfriend. It would have been nice to get to know him a little before he met the people I cared about. It all seemed a little rushed.

"I just signed up for the ice sculpting," my father said, pointing back toward the terrace. "I was pretty good at it in college, but it's been a few years. How about you, Kerri? Want to try your hand at some chiseling?"

I shook my head. "Art and I don't get along," I told him, trying to smile. Inside, my awkward feeling was growing. Why was he talking about ice sculpture when he was here to give me a check for college? *Give the guy some credit*, I reminded myself. Maybe he wanted to wait for some privacy before he gave me the money. But just the thought of being alone with my father made me even more nervous. I tried to focus on the conversation.

"We don't leave Kerri alone with sharp objects," Matt was saying with mock seriousness.

"Hey!" I punched him in the shoulder as my dad laughed.

"I'm going to do some sculpting," Erin said, joining us.

"She's the artistic one," I added, clapping Erin on the back. She was wearing a fake leopard-fur jacket with black leggings. Her purple combat boots were covered by fuzzy purple leg warmers. "Can't you tell? Do you remember Erin Yamada, Dad?"

"Oh, I remember," Dad said, shaking her hand. "Hard to forget the little girl who put blue food coloring in my swimming pool."

A big grin lit Erin's face. "You remember that? Cool!"

"And these are my other friends," I said as they walked up. "Maya. Her boyfriend, Luke. And Jessica."

"Jessie!" Dad took her hand and pulled her into his arms for a hug. "The last time I saw you, you were a beanpole. How are your parents?"

"Fine," Jessica said, beaming. Somehow, I'd never realized that she once sort of had a relationship with my dad too.

"I'd better go start that sculpture," Dad said. "They only give you three hours. I have a feeling I'll need every minute."

"Me too." Erin rubbed her hands together.

"We'll walk up with you," I said. As the group headed toward the tents, I thought about how strange the whole scene was. On the one hand, I was kind of happy that my father was there. I mean, he came all that way just to help me out. But on the other hand, he sort of just fit himself right back into my life. And my friends seemed to instantly accept him. He was kind of acting like he didn't disappear seven years ago. Like he'd been a real father to me all along. But he hadn't.

The more I thought about it, the more I began

to get angry. Did he think that he could erase everything that happened? Just because he was giving me some money?

My father turned to me. "You're kind of quiet," he said. "Maybe I should stay here with you and your friends instead of doing the ice sculpting."

I shook my head no. I had to sort through my feelings. I didn't want to say anything to my father that I would regret later. "You go ahead. I'll catch up with you later."

While Dad and Erin worked on their sculptures, the rest of us scattered off to different events. Matt and I competed in the ice slalom, but neither of us placed in the top three. About two hours later we headed into one of the heated tents.

"Hey, guys," Jessica called from the top of a metal picnic table. "Grab some hot chocolate and pull up a bench." She was sitting with Maya, Luke, and Glen, who seemed to be minus his girlfriend.

"Right now I'd like to dip my toes in cocoa," I said, dropping my skates under the table. My cheeks were stinging from the cold, but the warm tent filled with smells of chocolate and cinnamon rolls was warming me up already. "So who's doing what?"

"We've decided to drop out of the competitions and hang where it's really happening," Glen said. "By the food."

Matt grinned. "Sounds good to me."

We hung out, eating and joking. After a while I glanced around the tent, which was brimming with people. Mostly families, I noticed. My thoughts drifted back to my father.

He was so comfortable coming back to Madison, and I was so confused about him being here. Weren't fathers and daughters supposed to have some kind of special bond? Maybe. But I couldn't forget that *my* father had opted out of my life a long time ago. *Why?* I wondered. *Why did he do that? And why did he lie about where he was living?*

Feeling a twinge of sadness, I was about to say something to Matt, when Erin came into the tent, waving like mad.

"Get your butts out here!" she called to us. "They're judging the ice sculptures. Or do you want to miss it?"

Jessica let out a big sigh and rolled her eyes.

Erin stared at her. "I saw that, Jessica."

"Whatever," Jessica muttered.

"Hey, Jessica." Erin crossed the tent and stood next to her. "Shouldn't you be on *campus?*" she asked. "I mean, you're always telling us how much you like *campus*. What happened? Did your little campus friends dump you?"

Jessica's brows furrowed. Her mouth formed a thin line. She looked really pissed.

That was when I jumped in. "Down, girl," I said, slipping an arm around her shoulders. "I hate seeing my two best friends fight." I turned to Erin. "So come on. Show me your stuff."

Erin led me past an ice pig and a frozen pine tree to her creation. I gasped when I caught sight of it: a cluster of spiky stars, big and small, some seeming to explode out of others. The sharp, jutting edges caught the light, glittering and winking. "Awesome," I said.

"Thanks." Erin scraped a few shards of ice off the pedestal with her nail. "I was going to call it 'Starburst,' but that's so mundane. So I decided on 'Big Bang.'"

I nodded. "I like it."

"Cool!" Matt said from behind me as the rest of our friends caught up.

"A star is born!" Maya said. "Actually, it's more like ten . . . or twelve stars."

Glen circled it, studying the edges. "Nice work, Yamada. Too bad it'll be melted in a day or two. I mean, unless you have a really giant freezer. Ice is such a temporary medium."

"Thanks, Mr. Science," Erin teased him.

"So when do we find out who wins?" Jessica

asked impatiently.

"Don't know," Erin answered. "The judges have already made their rounds."

I stepped away from the group and looked toward the area where my father was working. I was about to head over and see what he was doing when I heard a high-pitched noise over the loudspeaker.

"Ladies and gentlemen," the announcer boomed a few seconds later, "the final scores are in for our ice-sculpting competition." The first prize went to that ridiculous pig. We clapped politely.

"Second prize goes to Erin Yamada for her brilliant 'Big Bang.'"

We all cheered and clapped as Erin executed a graceful bow, right down the to the toes of her boots.

"And an honorable mention goes to Michael Hopkins for his provocative 'Blind Liberty.'"

"Really?" Now I was very curious. "I've got to check this out," I told Erin.

Matt was right behind me as I cut through the crowd around my father. It was kind of hard to get close. Dad stood beside his sculpture, posing, making people laugh. I finally got a good look at Dad's work—the Statue of Liberty's head with a big hand over her eyes. A bright light went on, and I spotted the videocam. He was being interviewed by the local television news team!

"Can you lower those lights?" Dad teased, blocking his sculpture protectively. "A few more watts and this baby'll be one big puddle." Laughter rippled through the crowd, and Dad grinned again, soaking it up.

It reminded me of the way he stole the show at a school picnic when I was seven. Some of the dads had made ice cream, and my father was the one dishing it out. He made such a spectacle of the whole thing that kids and parents jumped back into line for more jokes, more laughs, more fun. Everyone always loved my dad.

"There she is!" Dad cried. Suddenly people turned to stare at me. "My daughter Kerri! The one who got me to try my hand at sculpting again." He leaned into the crowd, plucked me out, and led me into his circle of light and laughter and energy.

This was all too bizarre. To be on TV with my dad, swept up in his whole upbeat, life-is-super show. It was as if nothing had changed for him in all these years.

Part of me wanted to enjoy the moment, but the fact was that things *had* changed—*I'd* changed—a lot. I was practically an adult, and my father missed all the hard parts of growing up. Mom was the one who was there. Why should I totally let him back into my life now?

Dad squeezed my hand and then wrapped his arm around my shoulders as he smiled at the crowd. It felt . . . nice.

Maybe that's why, I thought, and squeezed back.

Then Dad pointed the reporters over to Erin. As they left, he turned to me. "I've got to call Sandy, just to check in."

My heart sank a little. For a moment I'd forgotten about his other family.

"Why don't you corral your friends and we'll head out to dinner," he went on. "You pick a place. Somewhere fun."

I nodded. "Thanks, Dad. My friends rarely turn down a free meal. I'll call Mom to let her know what I'm doing." I stepped away, then turned back. "Oh, and Dad . . . thanks for coming all the way to Madison to bring me my room deposit. I really appreciate it."

"Actually, I wanted to see you," he replied. "The money was just an excuse."

His response took me by surprise. "Uh . . . well, thanks," I said, and trudged off to find my friends. I wondered what my mom was going to say when I told her that Dad was in Madison. That he came to give me money for college—and to see me.

The crowd gravitated to Erin's sculpture, where she gestured dramatically for a reporter. I circled away from them and noticed Maya sitting alone on a big crate by one of the tents. I went over and joined her.

"My dad's invited us all out for dinner," I told her. "Do you think your father will let you go?"

Maya nodded, her dark eyes sad as she glanced into the shadows of the open tent.

I followed her gaze into the tent, where Maya's father stood beside Marlene, who held up a beaded necklace for his inspection. "Marlene's driving you nuts again?" I asked.

"They're getting really close," Maya said. "It feels like just yesterday when I found out they were seeing each other." She sighed. "Last night I think she slept over. Amanda was staying at her friend's house, and I saw Marlene and Dad watching the sunrise from the deck. She's been over early before, but never *that* early."

I gently touched Maya's shoulder. I didn't want to think about having my home invaded that way. Sure, I had Yucky Chucky to deal with, but he wasn't jumping into my father's boots.

Glancing over at the Indian jewelry booth, I noticed that Spencer and Marlene weren't shopping anymore. Marlene still held the necklace in one hand, but the other was securely planted on Spencer's chest. They looked like they were about to kiss.

"How sick is that!" Maya turned away from them. "My father would give me a major lecture if I did that with Luke. How can he not see what an idiot he's being?"

Trying to shake off a shiver, I kept patting Maya's shoulder. I couldn't imagine watching my dad kiss a strange woman. Maybe I wasn't ready for that family merger after all.

"Call me in the morning," Matt told me as he got up from the big, round table. "We'll do something, maybe in the afternoon." He and Luke were the last to leave True Blue Cheese, the restaurant near State Street where Dad treated my whole crew to a really fun dinner. Everyone else had already headed home, but Matt had suggested that he get a ride with Luke so that Dad and I could spend some time alone. That idea sounded nice for a Hallmark card but quite frankly planted a sick feeling in my stomach.

"Hold on a second," I said. Dad nodded as I put my napkin on the table and followed Matt out to the restaurant's foyer. "Don't leave me alone with him," I pleaded, grabbing his hands. "I don't know what to say to him!"

He shook his head. "It's been years, Kerri. I'm sure you have a few questions for your father," he said. "Go back there and be yourself. You're his daughter, and the fact that he's here means he wants to at least try. Give him a chance."

"But I wasn't expecting this," I complained. "I didn't plan out what to say."

"Even better. You can be totally spontaneous." He leaned down and gave me a kiss on the cheek. Then he was leaving, walking out the door, just like that.

Taking a deep breath, I went back to the dining room and sat across from my father. "And then there were two," I said lightly. But inside, my heart was racing a mile a minute.

I was about to ask my father questions. Questions I've had for a really long time. I just hoped I could handle the answers.

Chapter 11

"At last," Dad said, lifting his water glass. "We've never really had a chance to talk."

"No, we haven't," I said a little too hoarsely. I took a big gulp of water myself, trying to come up with a quick plan. How could I get the answers I needed without getting totally emotional about it?

"We have a lot of ground to cover, and some of it . . ." Dad paused. "Well, there's just no excuse for the parts of your life that I've missed. But there are a few things I want you to know. I don't know what your mother's told you, but it's important that you realize I wasn't the total bad guy in all this."

"Oh, right." I put my glass down so fast that water sloshed over the edge. "How can you say that? Like it was *good* that you disappeared?"

"Of course not, honey. But I always wanted to see you and Dan. I tried everything I could think of. But your mother always turned me away."

"What?" This was the first I'd heard of this. "That's not true. Mom told me she drove to Milwaukee to see you, and you turned *her* away."

"We argued," he admitted. "And after that she never gave me a chance. She thought that you'd be hurt to see me, that you'd feel torn between your two parents." He shook his head sadly. "Your mother did everything she could to convince me that you kids were better off without me. Not that I ever believed her. But after a while I gave up trying to get past her."

"But . . ." I shook my head. "Mom didn't . . . Why wouldn't she tell me that part?"

"She thought she was protecting you from me," he said.

I bit my lip thinking of what Mom said about my father when she found out I was e-mailing him. She said that Dad was a charmer. That she worried he'd drop in and out of my life. Worried that I'd get hurt. "I don't know," I said. "One minute you were moving to Arizona, the next we find out you're just miles away in Wisconsin."

"Which I thought you knew," he insisted. "Kerri, I sent letters to the apartment with my Milwaukee address. Your mother knew where I was, didn't she?"

I nodded. "But she didn't tell me anything until

a few months ago."

"I assumed that you and Dan knew I was back in Wisconsin too. I didn't realize how out of touch you were until the three of us connected through e-mails last fall. When I realized you thought I was still in Arizona, I . . . I didn't know what to do. I didn't want to upset you even more than I already had."

"But why didn't you call or write or something as soon as you moved back?" I asked. "You didn't even try."

"I did, I did. I told your mother, and I thought she told you. Can you imagine how I felt? I thought you knew I was living in Milwaukee, and I was hurt that you never tried to contact me. I never tried to hide. I'm in the phone book."

I stared at the table, a little shocked. The whole picture was becoming clear. There was my Dad wanting to see us. There were Dan and me, two kids, wishing he cared. And the messages never got through. All the tears, all the pain . . . was it really for nothing? Did he really care? Did he really want to be our father all along?

"Kerri . . ." His eyes shone in the dim light. Eyes that reminded me of my own. "I'd like to be a part of your life. That's why I kept e-mailing you even after you cut me off."

"And Dan," I said. "You've been e-mailing Dan. But you never came to see *him*."

Dad's jaw tightened for a second. "Dan . . ." He shrugged. "We do keep in touch through e-mail. But he's made it clear that he doesn't want to see me. I haven't given up on him yet, but I'm not going to force something he doesn't want."

I knew that Dan's feelings toward Dad were more complicated than he was letting on. I wiped the beads of condensation from my glass. I felt sorry for Dan. But at the same time I was struggling through my own emotions.

My fingers squeezed the hem of the tablecloth in my lap as I tried to absorb it all. I wanted to be angry with my mother for shielding us from Dad all these years. But I knew she was trying to do the right thing, trying to protect us from the husband she found to be so unpredictable, so unreliable.

I shook my head. "You think adults are doing the right thing just because they're adults."

"I know, Kerri. And I'm sorry."

I squeezed the tablecloth again. "You think your parents are perfect. You—you were always my hero."

A slow, sad smile lit his face. "Funny. Gabby tells me that now. You know, now that we've spent some time together, I'm really eager for you to meet Gabby and Sandy. Gabby's going to be thrilled to have a big sister."

Gabby? I shifted in my chair, a bit upset that he was bringing his new family into the conversation. The thought of his other daughter still made me squirm, and I wasn't sure how to get past that. Even worse, Dad had no idea it hurt me to hear about her.

"What?" Dad prodded. "What are you thinking?"

"Just that it can't be that easy to . . . I mean, can you really put a bunch of strangers together and make them a family?"

Dad reached across the table and squeezed my arm. "Absolutely."

"You sound so sure about that," I told him.

"It'll work out. You'll see," he said, glancing at his watch. "You'll drive up to Milwaukee for the weekend, and you'll feel like you've come home all over again."

I nodded, realizing that he had to get going. "I'll try to visit you soon. And thanks again for the trip down here. Especially with timing so tight on that room deposit."

"The check . . ." He stood and patted the pockets of his down jacket. "Oh, man. I could kick myself for driving down here without my checkbook." He slapped himself on the forehead.

I felt my heart sink. "Dad, you promised," I

said, hating the desperation in my voice. "The deadline is Thursday. What am I going to do?"

"I know, I'm an idiot. But don't worry. I'll put a check in the mail first thing tomorrow morning, okay?"

"Are you sure you'll remember?" I asked as my mother's warnings about Dad rushed through my head. *He's not dependable. He'll hurt you.* But I didn't want to think about that. I wanted to believe that my father would come through for me.

Dad paid the check, then followed me out of the restaurant to where my car was parked. "You're nervous again," he said. "I can tell."

I shrugged. "Yeah, well, it's important to me."

"As it should be." He touched my shoulder, flashing me his big trademark smile. "I'm going to come through for you, honey. Don't worry. I won't let you down."

Chapter 12

"**H**ow did it go?" my mother asked as soon as I walked through the door to our apartment. She was sitting on the couch. A deck of tarot cards was spread out on the coffee table in front of her.

"Weird," I said. I told her about how my father showed up at the winter festival. About the dinner and the talk we had afterward.

"I have to admit," Mom said. "I didn't think he'd come down here with a check."

"Well . . ." I hesitated. "He accidentally left his checkbook at home. But he's going to put it in the mail first thing tomorrow."

Mom let out a heavy sigh. "Kerri, he's not going to come through with the money."

That was the last thing I wanted to hear. "Mom, aren't you the one who's always saying that negative thoughts breed negative actions?"

"Yes, but—"

"Then stop being so negative!" I exclaimed.

Mom gathered her tarot cards into a neat pile. "Look, Kerri, I know your father," she said, surprising me with a harsh tone. "He probably doesn't want to tell you that he can't give you the money, so he's stalling. Then pretty soon it'll be too late. You won't have the money for Miami, and you won't have applied to any other schools. Then what are you going to do?"

I rose from the couch and crossed the room to the closet. "You obviously know more than I do about Dad," I replied, taking off my jacket and putting it away. "How come you never told me the whole truth?" I asked. "How come you never said he wanted to see me and Dan?" I knew it wasn't fair to bring that up now, but I didn't want to answer her question.

"You know I was protecting you and Dan!" she yelled. "Maybe you don't remember waiting for hours, then crying yourself to sleep when he didn't show up. But I do. I was there!"

I didn't know what to say. I'd never seen my mother so upset before. Could she be jealous of Dad? Afraid I'd learn to love him again? "Mom, calm down," I told her. "Take a cleansing breath or something."

"Don't tell me to calm down!" she cried. She was about to scream something else, but instead she sat down on the couch again. She ran a hand through her shoulder-length blond hair and leaned back. "I'm sorry. Now I know why I gave up yelling. It's such a waste of energy." She paused. "This is about your future, Kerri," she said in a tone more like herself. "I brought home some more college catalogs. SUNY Buffalo has a great PT program. Just think about applying, okay?"

"Fine. I'll apply to a few other schools," I said to get her off my back. But just because my mother was feeling jealous, that didn't mean I had to give up my dream. And it didn't mean that my father wouldn't keep his promise. *Positive thoughts . . .*

On Monday Matt and I checked the mail as soon as we got to my apartment after school. Of course there was no check from my father.

"Even if he mailed the letter Saturday night, it wouldn't arrive by today," Matt pointed out as we sifted through junk mail.

"Tomorrow," I said, putting Mom's stack of bills on the kitchen table.

The next day I drove home from school thinking very positive thoughts. Dad's check would arrive today. I would drive it right over to the bank and deposit it. I would write a check to the University of Miami and mail it on the spot. I imagined Dad's envelope with one of those self-stick return address labels in the corner. I was getting into that whole visualization thing—one of my mom's New Age pursuits.

I parked my car and ran across the parking lot. The letter would be there. Mail from Milwaukee was usually fast. Overnight would be no big deal. I keyed open the mailbox and saw three crisp envelopes inside. Two letters for Mom and one for me.

But the return address was the University of Miami. A sick feeling crept back in my stomach. I tore open the envelope out in the cold afternoon wind and saw that it was a reminder. A reminder that the room deposit was due this week—Thursday. As if I needed a reminder.

Okay, okay, I told myself, *maybe you're stressing out over nothing.* What did Matt suggest the other day? Call the university and get an extension. A great idea. Reduced stress was just a phone call away.

I bounded up the stairs to the apartment. "I'm home!" I called, waiting for an answer from Dan. When the place was silent, I guessed that he was out. Probably at a movie with his friends. I wondered if Dan's business was really ever going to take off or if he'd spend the rest of his life living in his old bedroom in Mommy's apartment. Hard to tell, but one thing was for sure: I wasn't going to follow in his footsteps. Come September, I'd be out of here.

As I dropped Mom's mail on the kitchen table, I spotted a note. I picked it up.

> Kerri—
> Don't forget—applications for most colleges are due by the end of this week. Did you send them out already? Thanks for humoring me.
> Love, M

I know I said I would apply to other schools, but I didn't mean it. My mind was set. Miami, and that was that. Positive thoughts. I'd make it work. I crumpled the paper and dropped it into the recycle bin. Bye-bye.

Inside my room I dug through the packet from the University of Miami and found the number of the bursar's office. Why should they care if I sent their money this week or next month? Thousands of students came through those doors every semester. One measly payment from me wasn't going to make any difference to them.

I grabbed the phone and tapped in the number. The woman who answered had a slight Spanish accent. When she asked my name, she sounded helpful, even friendly. She found my name in the computer and verified that they were holding a room for me.

"I was just wondering if I could get an extension

on the deadline for the deposit," I said. "I mean, I'm definitely attending in the fall, but I'm not sure I'll be able to get the check out in time."

"Oh, no, honey, no extensions," she said in a low voice. "Sorry, but nobody can help you with that. We're not allowed to play with the deadlines." And that ended our call.

Okay, I thought, sucking in my breath through my teeth. *Time to panic is NOW.*

I put down the phone and tapped my fingernails against the shiny catalog. What if Dad's check didn't get here by tomorrow? The sick feeling in my stomach was getting worse. I couldn't sit around here and do nothing while my whole college career slipped away.

I jumped up and grabbed my jacket and keys. Matt might have another idea.

"You look awful," I said when Matt answered the door. Maybe it wasn't the kindest thing to say, but one look at his pale face and the words just popped out. "Are you feeling okay?"

"Not really," he said, handing me a crisp folded piece of paper. "Today's my day for bad news."

I skimmed the letter, which announced that he was being offered early admission to Purdue, along with a full football scholarship. I squinted up at him.

"This is the bad news?"

"Shh," he said, nodding toward the living room.

I glanced in and saw his mom sitting on the piano bench, talking on the cordless phone. Noticing me, she smiled. I waved back and followed Matt into the kitchen.

"Mom is psyched," he said. "She hasn't been off the phone since I opened the letter. Everyone she knows has to hear the big news." He sat down at the kitchen table and lowered his head into his hands. "My life is over."

I slid the letter onto the kitchen table, trying not to stare at the words "full scholarship." Okay, I felt a little jealous. Jealous of something Matt didn't even want.

He raked his hands through his hair without looking up at me. "I feel so trapped. Locked in."

"Look, I know Purdue isn't your first choice, but—"

"No, it's my parents' choice," he said, cutting me off. "And if I go there, which is a given now, I'll have to play football. Do you know how time-consuming that is in college? I've seen the deal with my older brother. He has to go to a special study hall every night. He's got to dorm and eat with the other team members. It's like going to Football U."

"I know, I know," I said softly. "But Purdue is a good school. And I'm sure you can take some music classes. Why don't you think of the scholarship as a way to get what *you* want?"

"Why are you pushing me to go to Purdue?" Matt glared at me. "I thought at least you'd understand." He shook his head. "I mean, you don't want to go anywhere but Miami, and you can't even afford it!"

"Why are you angry with *me?*" I asked. "What did *I* do to you?"

"You don't get it," he said, rubbing his eyes. "They've got college all mapped out for me. I'm stuck doing what they want. Locked into four years of football and some boring degree like business or prelaw."

But I did get it. I did know what it was like to see your dream slipping out of your reach. But in my case, I couldn't do anything about it. "Matt," I said gently. "Talk to your parents. Maybe they'll understand."

"I told you," Matt said. "I can't let them down."

I felt bad for him, but I knew that wouldn't help. This was something Matt had to handle on his own. If he wasn't going to talk to his parents, I couldn't push him to do it.

"Well, look at the bright side," I said, reaching across the table to touch his hand. "You're not going to be stuck at Purdue every weekend. And did you know that Miami has some great clubs? And music? There's a huge Cuban influence. We'll check it out when you visit for Miami's homecoming, and then—"

"Stop it!" He slid his hand out from under mine, then banged it on the table. "You can't plan my life too!"

I stared at him. I'd never seen Matt lose his temper, and I'd never expected him to lose it with me.

"Who knows how we'll feel when we get to college?" he went on. "We'll probably want some time to ourselves just to chill and meet new people. You can't figure out our lives on a little calendar."

Meet new people? The words rang in my ears. "What do you mean by 'meet new people'?"

Matt didn't answer. He glanced at me, then turned away.

"Are you saying you want to *see* other people in college?" I asked. "As in other *girls?*"

"Well, no. I don't know. Who knows what'll happen once we're apart?"

I didn't know what to say next. How long had Matt been feeling this way? I had no idea, but I did know that I couldn't let him see how much he'd just hurt me.

"You are so right," I said, looking away to hide my expression, "I might want to date other guys, and you'll probably want to see other girls."

I managed to get the words out with a casual shrug, but inside I didn't feel so calm and casual.

Inside, my heart was breaking.

Chapter 13

I made it out of Matt's house and into my car with some mumbled excuse about homework or something equally lame. The inside door panel separated from the rest of the car as I pulled the door shut. Great. My car was falling apart, just like my life. I turned the key, drove to the nearest phone booth, and called Jess.

"Jessica is at the UW library," her mother told me. "Something about another group project."

"Thanks, Mrs. Carvelli," I said, feeling so alone. I hung up and called Maya's private line. When her machine picked up, I called her cell phone.

Maya picked up on the second ring.

"I need you guys—now," I said as tears began to stream down my face.

"Oh, God! Are you okay?" I could hear the concern in Maya's voice.

"Not really," I replied, my voice quivering.

"Can you meet me at Applewhite's restaurant in the mall?" Maya asked. "I'm here with Erin."

"I'll be there," I said. "Just give me ten minutes or so."

Inside the restaurant I spotted Maya and Erin sitting in a back booth. I walked past the walls covered with movie posters, tennis rackets, funky hats, and weird sculptures.

Erin turned toward me. "Kerri! Come, sit, talk."

"We were so worried," Maya said as I slid into the seat beside her.

I slumped over the table. "I can't believe this is happening to me," I said.

"What happened?" Erin asked.

"I don't know how it started, but I went over to Matt's house this afternoon. He found out that he got early admission to Purdue—with a full scholarship. I know it sounds great, but he's bummed since it's not really his dream. Anyway, I was just trying to cheer him up about it when he freaked and told me not to plan anything for next year, as in planning that we'll be together. He said that—" My voice broke. I tried not to cry again. "He said we might be seeing other people by then."

Maya gasped. Even Erin seemed surprised.

"You and Matt?" Maya asked. "Why would you break up? You guys are so perfect together."

Perfect together. That's what I thought. Apparently not what Matt's been thinking. Suddenly hot tears filled my eyes. Before I could say another word, teardrops were rolling down my face. I felt warm and sick and out of control. "Am I losing him?" I asked aloud. "I don't know what I did."

"Oh, Kerri." Maya hugged me close, patting my back. "This is so not fair. It's definitely not your fault."

"The guy loves you," Erin insisted. She handed me a packet of tissues from her coat pocket. "Maybe he's just temporarily insane about this Purdue thing."

"I don't know." I kept seeing the way Matt banged the table. The flash of anger in his eyes. At the time it seemed to be about me. "Do you really think he could get that freaked out about college?"

"Hello?" Erin said, pretending to knock on my head. "Haven't you spent just about every minute of the past few days stressing about the room deposit for Miami? College is a major freak-out. And it's going to get worse. You guys put in for early admission. Wait until the rest of us start getting letters." She shook her head. "No. I'm not going to stress over it. If I get in somewhere, I get in. If not, then I'll travel the world."

"I just hate not knowing where I want to go and what schools will accept me," Maya said.

"That's why I'm applying to fifteen schools. I've got all the forms filled out, and I'm almost finished with the essays. I figure at least one of them has to let me in."

Maya's wide eyes were so sincere that I smiled through my tears. "I wonder if that's it, that Matt is stressed about college. I know it's been killing me. I still didn't get the check from my father."

"See?" Erin pointed at me. "Major college anxiety."

"And I called Miami, but I can't get an extension," I added.

Erin winced. "Did you call your dad to see what's up?"

I shook my head. "He promised to mail it out. I have to wait."

"Talk about a bad day," Maya said, hugging me again. "But don't worry. I'm sure your father's check will be in tomorrow's mail. And Matt's going to apologize next time you see him."

Maya sounded so sure of herself that I almost believed her. Almost.

On Wednesday morning I saw Matt outside the gym. He nodded at me, but his attention was focused on his friends, who were joking about how some guy got scammed into buying a worthless car.

They all thought it was extremely funny, but I couldn't laugh. Didn't Matt realize we had more important things to talk about? I thought about pulling him aside, but I could imagine the comments his friends would make, things like "Fowler is whipped!" or "What's the four-one-one on that leech?"

At lunchtime we sat together at our usual table. Eating a spoonful of yogurt, I studied him, wondering what was going on in his head. As he sat back with his sandwich and waved at someone across the cafeteria, I couldn't stop the anger that began to burn inside me. He was acting like nothing had happened yesterday—nothing at all!

I wanted to jump up on the lunchroom table and shout, "What's wrong with you? Apologize already! Take it back! Tell me you really *don't* want to see other people!"

How could he sit there like that?

I took a deep breath and tried to pull myself together. Okay, I was worried about the college money. Today was Wednesday. The deposit had to be postmarked by tomorrow. And I was freaked that Matt mentioned seeing other people. But the pressure of both of those problems was really getting to me. I had to get out of there before I exploded.

"I just remembered," I said as I got up and put the lid on my yogurt. "I promised Erin I'd help her with something backstage."

Matt nodded. "Yup."

"We'll talk later?" I asked. "Meet me by my locker after school, okay?"

He nodded again, not exactly bubbling over with enthusiasm. Clutching my lunch things to my chest, I bit my lip. It was the only way I could keep myself from crying.

I spent the afternoon stressing over Matt and the check from my father. When the final bell rang, I went to my locker and waited for Matt. The halls began to empty, but still he didn't turn up. Not sure what to think, I slammed my locker closed and headed out. Maybe he was just tied up somewhere, but I couldn't wait around all afternoon. I had to get home and check the mail.

I was passing the main office when I saw Jessica by the double doors. "Jess! What are you doing here?" She spent just about every afternoon on the University of Wisconsin campus.

"My communications class was canceled, and I figured I'd swing back here to talk to my guidance counselor." Jessica looked at me suspiciously. "Where's Matt?"

"I wish I knew," I said, holding back the tears.

"Did you guys talk about it?" Jessica knew the whole story. I'd reached her on the phone the previous night.

I shook my head.

"Come on. I'll help you find him."

I shook my head again. "I can't wait around. I've got to get home and pick up the mail. I need to grab Dad's check and get that deposit out."

"Oh, right," Jessica said. "Tomorrow's the deadline."

I nodded. "And I have to admit, I'm feeling a little desperate. About everything."

"No wonder." She hitched her backpack over her shoulder. "The guidance counselor can wait. Let's go."

Jessica followed me in her car back to my place. As soon as we parked, we headed straight to the apartment building's mailboxes.

"Come on, come on. I know you're here," I whispered as I reached into the mail slot and pulled out a stack of letters. "Elizabeth Hopkins . . . Elizabeth Hopkins . . ." They were all addressed to my mother—every last one.

"Dad's check isn't here," I told Jess. My pulse started to race.

"Okay, don't panic," she said. "He can always wire you the money. Why don't you call him and find out if and when he sent it out?"

"Right." We both ran up the stairs to the apartment. I grabbed the phone while Jess dumped the mail on the table. Still wearing my coat and backpack, I punched in my father's phone number and waited as it rang. There was a click and then a recorded message: "We're not here right now, but if you'd like to leave your name and number, we'll—"

I hung up. "I got the machine." I covered my face with my hands. "I can't take it! What are the chances that Dad's check will make it in time? By tomorrow?"

Jessica leaned against the kitchen wall. "Okay, then. What's plan B?"

"Plan B? There is no plan B!" I paced across the kitchen, then stopped. "But there could be an alternate plan." I ran into my room and opened the wooden junk box sitting on my dresser. There I found my green ATM card and some bank statements. Jessica and I had opened our first savings accounts together back when we were kids.

"Your savings account?" Jessica asked from the doorway. "Do you have enough money in it?"

"Probably not, but I've been banking all my birthday money, plus all the cash I made working at Bernie's." I sifted through the papers in the box to find the latest account report. Jessica moved to my side as I found the last balance. "Fifteen hundred sixty-two dollars," I read aloud. "Yeah! I can't believe I have this much money in my account!"

Jess nudged my arm. "We knew you weren't slinging bagels at Bernie's for nothing!"

"This is like a really huge moment," Jessica said, leaning over the counter beside me as I made out the withdrawal slip. Although I had an ATM card, I needed to go to the bank to have a check drawn on my savings account. "I should have brought my camera." She pretended to frame my face in a photo. "This is Kerri taking out her life savings for college."

I pretended to smile for the camera, then continued filling in my account number.

Jessica gave me a thumbs-up as we stepped into the line. The arrow pointed to a teller window, and we hurried over. I slid the withdrawal slip under the glass and looked at Jessica. Suddenly we both burst out laughing. It was such a weird exciting moment. Behind the glass the teller tapped away at her computer.

"After you mail everything off, we'll go celebrate," Jessica promised. "We can head over to the Empty Cup. A lot of the kids from campus hang out there. My treat."

"Good," I teased, "because I'm going to be broke."

She laughed again, but her smile faded as the teller called my name.

"Ms. Hopkins?"

I swung around to see the teller holding up the withdrawal slip.

"I'm sorry," the woman said, sliding the slip back to me. "But the balance in your account doesn't cover this withdrawal."

I glanced at the numbers she'd written on the slip: "Current balance: $1,242.13."

"This is impossible," I said. "How can I be three hundred dollars short?"

Chapter 14

"This can't be right," I told the teller. "My last statement said I have more than fifteen hundred dollars in my account."

"Let's see." The teller clicked away at her computer keyboard. "There was a withdrawal of twenty dollars last week."

I thought back. "Oh, right. At the cash machine." I turned to Jessica. "They were having a sale at Express."

"And another on the twelfth," the teller added. She kept typing, then looked up at me. "I'll print the list for you."

"The list?" A moment later she handed me a sheet of itemized ATM withdrawals, each for twenty dollars. "Oh," I said sadly as I scanned the list. "I forgot to record the money I took out of cash machines." Those withdrawals really added up.

"Oh, no!" Jessica frowned.

I was out of money and out of luck. Even my last attempt to save myself had failed. A painful lump formed in my throat. *Oh, please, don't start crying in the bank!* I told myself.

"Okay, okay," I said, feeling like an idiot as I backed away from the teller's window. "Sorry," I told her.

"Wait," Jessica said, grabbing my elbow. "You're so close, Ker. I'll lend you the difference."

"Three hundred dollars?" I looked at her backpack. "You have three hundred dollars?"

"In my account, you idiot." Jessica leaned close to the teller's window. "Can you give us two more withdrawal slips? I don't know how you want to work it, but she'll need one bank check from two different accounts."

"You're the best!" I told Jess, feeling a little embarrassed. "I'll never forget this, and I'll pay you back right away. As soon as Dad's check comes."

"Don't worry about it," Jess teased. "I know where to find you."

I smiled, but I wished I could stop worrying.

With a crisp money order for fifteen hundred dollars in my hands, I pushed open the door of the bank and led the way out to State Street. I had the whole packet, along with some preregistration forms and room requests, all filled out and ready to go.

At the post office I slid all the papers and the check into one of the red, white, and blue cardboard envelopes for Priority Mail. I sealed the envelope and then gave it a big, fat kiss. It was a deposit on my future.

After everything I'd been through that week, it felt so good to see the postal clerk drop that envelope into his canvas bag. "Miami, here I come," I said.

"You're lucky to know where you're going," Jessica told me as we walked out of the post office. "I wish I knew if I was going to NYU, but it's such a guessing game. So I'm working on six applications."

"Six! You and Maya are nuts. And why wouldn't you get into NYU? You have excellent grades. You'll even have college credit from the University of Wisconsin."

Jess shrugged. "Maybe I'm just insecure. The fact that I bombed that sociology final at the U doesn't help. And even if I get into NYU, I need a scholarship too."

"I guess college is stressing everyone," I said. Packed snow crunched under our feet as we veered off the sidewalk and hiked over a snowbank toward the Empty Cup Café. We'd had a few feet of snow in the past week, and there was more in the forecast for this weekend.

"Just think. Next year when I come home for semester break, I'll be flying from bikini weather to snow. Is that cool or what?"

"Very." Checking her reflection in the glass window of the Empty Cup, Jessica pulled off her beret and raked back her long, dark hair.

"Jess! You're primping! You never used to fuss like that."

"Just checking," she replied. "Besides, this is a campus hangout. Got to look good, right? You never know who you're going to meet."

"You always look good. It's just funny to see you cruising yourself in a shop window." Staring through the glass, I noticed the crowd of students kicking back inside. One guy had his boots off, his red-toed socks propped up on a couch. There was a girl with her head in her boyfriend's lap. Students reading newspapers or talking on cell phones or having dramatic conversations. Altogether the vibe was different from a get-together of kids from South Central High. This was definitely U territory.

"There's Jake from last semester's sociology class. And Athena and Zoe from English." Jessica waved through the glass, then led the way through the café door. Warm air laden with rich coffee smells hit me as I stepped inside. I followed her over to a couch full of students, feeling like a little kid.

"Hey, guys," she said, stuffing her beret into a pocket. "What's up?"

"Not much," a girl with rectangular blue glasses answered. She eyed me curiously but didn't say anything. "What's up with you, Jessica?"

From there the conversation got into things about classes and teachers and assignments at the university. I wandered over to the end of the coffee line. I looked at the menu on a chalkboard behind the counter.

Jessica joined me just as I got to the front of the line. "Sorry about that. Zoe is really freaked about a paper we're all doing."

We took our drinks over to a small table by the window and tossed our jackets over the backs of the chairs. I sat down and scooped up a spoonful of delicious whipped cream. Across from me Jessica was stirring sugar into her cappuccino when she glanced up and spotted someone. Probably another student from campus, I assumed, until I saw the way her face lit up.

"Alex!" She stood and went back toward the counter. "Hi! What are you doing here?"

I turned around and saw Alex McKay striding in from the cold, unwrapping a knit scarf. His chin lifted, and he paused as his eyes flashed on Jess.

"How've you been?" Jessica asked, pushing her hair back nervously.

Alex stared at Jessica. Actually, he stared right through her. "You know? Suddenly I'm not thirsty anymore." He tossed his scarf back over his shoulder and headed out the door.

Jessica stood there frozen for a minute. Then she swung around toward me, her face sullen.

I motioned her back to our table. I knew that Alex was still angry with her, but there was no reason to treat her that way.

"He hates me," Jessica said, her eyes wide with pain. "He really hates me. He won't even talk to me, all because of Erin."

"You can't blame her completely," I said. "I mean, Alex isn't exactly being mature about this whole thing."

Jess shook her head. "Well, I guess I deserve it."

"People make mistakes," I told her. We'd been over this, dozens of times, and I felt bad for Jess. She never meant to fool around with Scott Seifert behind Alex's back—it just sort of happened. "But I've been meaning to talk to you about this. You've got to stop blaming Erin."

"I can't help it," Jessica said. "I was this close to getting back together with Alex." She held her fingers so close that a speck of dust wouldn't fit between them. "And Erin had to open her big mouth."

"Don't you see how much it bothers her every time you throw it in her face?" I asked. "She made a mistake. You've got to let it go. Focus on Alex. How can you get him to be your friend again?"

Jessica pushed her coffee cup away and folded her arms. "I don't know. I've tried everything. It's hopeless."

"Don't say that," I said, suddenly thinking of Matt. Exactly where did we stand? Since our argument he'd been distant. Not exactly the guy I'd fallen in love with. We really needed to talk. I scanned the café for a pay phone. There were two on the wall by a coatrack just a few feet from our table. I searched my pockets for change. "Do you have any change? I'd better call Matt. Now that I've taken care of the Miami deadline, I think I can talk to him without losing it."

Jessica handed me two quarters. "So you're going to call him and what? Give him another chance to apologize?"

"You can still read my mind," I said, going over to the phone on the wall. "But if he doesn't take the bait, I'll try to set up a time to talk. I think he's been avoiding me at school." I punched in Matt's number and held my breath.

"Hello?" his mother answered.

When I said my name and asked for Matt, she warmed up. I guessed Matt hadn't told her about our fight.

"Matt's not here right now," she said. "He's down the street, working on a school project at Genna's house."

"Project?" I repeated. But I was thinking, Who's Genna? Then, not wanting to sound jealous and suspicious, I added, "Oh, that project. Okay, Mrs. Fowler. Thanks. I'll talk to you soon."

Jessica was staring at me as I dropped back into the chair. "What did he say?" she asked.

"He wasn't home," I answered, trying to remember Matt's classes. "His mom said he's working on a class project. Do you know any Gennas?"

She nodded. "Genna Reed, a senior. On the yearbook staff. You've seen her around. Red hair. Kind of pretty."

I had a bad feeling about this Genna girl. Very bad. I didn't want to be jealous, but after our fight I couldn't help it.

What if Matt didn't wait until college? What if he was *already* seeing someone else?

Chapter 15

That night when Mom got home from work, I told her that Jess and I had mailed off the room deposit.

"Your father sent the check?" she asked, taking off her jacket and hanging it in the closet.

I hesitated. Then I lied. "Yup. It came today." I didn't want to get another lecture on how my father wasn't reliable.

"I'm so glad I was wrong about your father," my mother said, giving me a big hug. "And I'm sorry about being so negative. I know Miami is the school you really wanted."

"It's okay," I said, adding spaghetti to a pot of boiling water. Although we rarely ate dinner together, I had decided to cook up a little celebration meal. Spaghetti and salad were manageable enough without stretching my culinary skills.

"And you're making dinner." Mom stood

behind me, pulling my hair back over my shoulders. "What am I going to do without you next year? It's going to be quiet around here."

"Don't worry," I said, stirring the pasta. "You'll still have Dan."

"But I'll miss you," she said. "Let me change out of these clothes and I'll help you." She turned to leave and then stopped. "Oh, did you mail off the other college applications too? Most of them are due this week."

"What for?" I asked. "It's all set. I'm going to Miami."

Mom sighed. "It's better to be safe than sorry," she replied. "You never know what might happen. At least apply to the University of Wisconsin."

"Maybe," I said, trying to tune her out.

After dinner I felt a little sorry for myself as I sat down at the computer. Here I was, all set to go off to my dream college, and I couldn't even tell my boyfriend about it. Actually, I wasn't even sure I *had* a boyfriend if Matt really was sneaking around with Genna what's-her-name.

I logged onto the Internet and started an e-mail to my father. I needed to say, "Send me that stupid check, already!" But in a nice way.

Hey, anybody home? You know, I still didn't

get your check today. (The post office is fired!)
But since I couldn't reach you, I went ahead and
sent off the deposit, but I had to scrape it
together with a loan from Jessica. Anyway, I'm
good for now. I just hope that check comes
soon. I promised I'd pay back Jessica ASAP!!!
   —Kerri

Then I started an e-mail to Matt. What could I
say? I decided to keep it simple.

Hello in there? Called you today, but you
were out. Can we talk?
   Love, Kerri

After that I drummed my fingers over the
keyboard, wondering if I should update Maya and
Erin on everything. But-*BING!* Almost immediately,
a new e-mail came in.

It was from Dad.

Kerri—Hey, that's great news. I've been out
of town on business, so I didn't get a chance to
send the check out.

Well, thanks for letting me know, I thought,
then continued to read.

Nice of Jessica to come through with a loan. Don't worry—I'll give you the check as soon as I see you. Which reminds me. Can you come up this weekend? Gabby is dying to meet you, and Sandy says that any time is fine. Let me know. And would you ask Dan if he'd like to come along? He's certainly welcome.

—Dad

The thought of meeting my father's other daughter made me a little nervous. I glanced at the calendar on the wall. I could say that I had to study for midterms this weekend. But the idea of having that check in my hands made me think twice, especially since I needed to pay Jessica back. I decided to go for it, but I didn't want to go for it alone.

This weekend looks good for me. How about Saturday afternoon? Is it okay to bring a friend or two? We'll stay till Sunday so we all have time to hang together. I hope you've warned Gabby that I'm not five and I don't do dolls anymore.

—K

I took a deep breath and clicked Send. It was

done. I was going to meet the other family. No turning back allowed.

Feeling restless, I spun my chair away from the screen. My senior chemistry textbook lay open on my desk, waiting for me to study. Beside it was the messy stack of applications and brochures from the colleges I was supposed to apply to—according to my mom. I thought about Jessica and Maya applying to ten colleges out of fear of rejection. What a waste of time.

I picked up a brochure from the University of Wisconsin, then tossed it into the recycle bin. A catalog from Wagner College showed the Manhattan skyline. *Not for me*, I thought.

In one broad sweep I pushed all the college papers into the recycle bin. I crunched it down with my foot, then hid the basket under my desk. After it was done, I felt good. Strong. Solid. I knew where I was going.

And my desk looked a whole lot cleaner.

Now it was time to start an e-mail to my friends to persuade them to go on another road trip to Milwaukee.

Hey, chicks!
Strap on your helmets and get in gear for a
fun-filled trip to the booming metropolis of

Milwaukee. Dad's invited one and all for an
overnight this Saturday. Okay, he just invited
me, and I asked if you guys could come, but I'm
sure it's okay. It's just that I don't want to be
stuck in a room alone with "the other family."
It'll be too weird. Who's in?

LYLAS, Kerri

I addressed the e-mail to Jessica, Erin, and
Maya, and then clicked Send. I stayed online as I
bent over my textbook and focused on biology
homework for a few minutes.

BING! Incoming.

I opened an e-mail from Jessica.

Sorry, sister, but I can't make the road trip.
Got a college paper due. Big whine. I wish I
could be there for you.

But good news on the Fowler front. I asked
around, and it turns out that Genna Reed IS in
Matt's history class, and they DO have a group
project due next week. Hey, these research
skills come in handy, right?

Love ya, Jess

I sank back into my chair and covered my face
with my hands. What a relief!

I wrote back to Jess:

> **Big sigh! Thanks for staying on my case, Detective Carvelli. And hey, double thanks for the loan. You saved my skin, sis!**

I clicked Send. But while I was writing, two e-mails had come in. It looked like everyone was online tonight. Must have been a boring night for homework assignments. The first message was from Maya:

> **Milwaukee sounds great, but Dad won't let me do an overnight. I don't want to push him. Got to save the big fights for the big battles, right? Anyway, this is a good thing, you and your dad together for a family visit. I'm really happy for you, Kerri.**

The second e-mail was from Erin:

> **Road trip! Gotta love it. Send details!**

As I was reading Erin's message, the doorbell rang. "Oh, hi!" I heard my mother say out in the living room. "Kerri! It's Matt!"

Matt? Here? I swallowed hard as I hurried out

to the living room. Matt stood there, his hands stuck in his jeans pockets, looking awkward. "It's good to see you, Matt," Mom said, tactfully heading off to her room to give us some privacy. She must have sensed that something was up. The air was thick with tension.

"I've been trying to call you," he said. "You and Dan must both be online."

He's been trying to call me, I thought. *Good. He wants to apologize.* "I'm glad you came over," I said, smiling. I dropped onto the couch and motioned for him to sit beside me. "You've been such a stranger the past few days."

"Yeah." Matt sat on the rattan chair across from the couch. It seemed like forever before he'd even look at me. Finally he did. "Kerri, there's something I've got to tell you," he said seriously. "There's a reason I haven't been around lately."

My smile faded. This wasn't sounding like an apology.

Chapter 16

I stared into Matt's eyes, trying to guess what horrible news he was about to tell me.

"I stayed away because I was thinking. I needed to mellow out," he said. "And I guess I need you to mellow out too."

"Me?" I heard my voice crack. "I'm mellow. Totally kicked back."

"No, you're not," Matt said. "It's not that it's a bad thing. But I like to live for the moment. Worry about the details later."

"Me too!" I insisted. "That's the way I am too."

Matt shook his head no. "Your life is already booked through next January! And you're getting more and more intense about everything. And . . . it's freaking me out."

I was freaking *him* out? He had to be kidding me. "What are you trying to tell me?" I asked him.

He didn't answer. He just shook his head.

I had a horrible feeling I knew where this was going. "Do you want to break up with me?"

"No," Matt said. "I don't think so . . . I don't know." He leaned forward and rubbed his palms on the knees of his jeans.

"You don't *know*?" I asked.

"Can't we just take things as they come?" he asked. "Can't you stop making plans for us? Sit back and enjoy the here and now."

I swallowed. I thought I was enjoying the here and now.

"Do you think you can do that?" he asked.

"Yeah. Sure." I shrugged, trying to keep things casual. But as I watched Matt leave, the truth hit me hard. Our relationship was crumbling. And I didn't know what to do to stop it.

"It's so unfair," I told Jess, who was about to head off to the university for afternoon classes. We were standing in front of my locker. "You try to plan a few things that will be fun, and you get accused of being too intense." I'd explained the whole Matt saga to her last night. "And here it is, lunchtime, and he's nowhere in sight. What's that about?"

Jessica leaned against a locker. "I don't know," she said. "You're talking to someone who's been trying to win back a guy since before Christmas. I'm no expert. Hey, look who's coming."

I spun around and spotted Matt, carrying his guitar case.

"Hey, Kerri . . . Jessica." He walked up to us and paused, looking a little awkward. "I've got to get over to the music wing. My buds are waiting for me."

"For what?" I asked.

"See you guys later," Jessica said, backing away. "Got to get to the U. Professor Kazorowski waits for no one."

As I watched her go, I longed for the old days when Jess was in school with me all day long. I missed her.

"Anyway, I've got this rehearsal," Matt said, "so I guess I'll catch you later." He started down the hall.

"Wait!" I called. "Rehearsal for what?"

"For our gig at the Cellar this weekend." He squinted at me. "I thought I told you about it. I'm playing with Larry and John, but we need to rehearse, and Mr. Calvert agreed to let us use the music room as long as we keep things low-key."

"Oh." I nearly choked out the word. I was sure he hadn't told me about the gig, and now I wondered why. Had he been trying to hide it?

"Well, I'm late already," he said, turning away. "Later."

"'Bye." Leaning my hot cheek against the cool

gray door of my locker, I watched as he headed down the hall. My heart was breaking. Why didn't he invite me to hang out and listen while he rehearsed? Didn't he want me with him? Didn't he know that I wanted us to stay together?

Apparently Matt didn't feel the same way anymore.

"Who can say how a guy feels?" Erin said as she peeled an orange with a red glittery thumbnail. She was sitting on the conference table in Mr. Calvert's office. Erin had a lot of clout in the backstage area. And today we were eating our lunch there.

Maya and I sat in chairs as the three of us picked at our lunches and philosophized about the terrible way Matt was acting.

"I say Matt is in the dark," Maya said. "Something is bothering him, maybe the news about Purdue. But whatever it is, it's making him blind to the good things in his life. Like Kerri."

I wondered if Maya was right. I wasn't sure.

"Hey, Erin," called a male voice.

We all turned to look out through the windowed wall of Mr. Calvert's office to the theater department's rehearsal room beyond. A few other students stood in a cluster.

"They must be finished practicing for the play," Erin said, licking her fingers.

A tall, dark, gorgeous guy dressed in jeans, a sweater, and a cape appeared in the doorway. "Lady Erin . . . whither thou goest?" I recognized Brandon Slavin, the student who usually played the tall, dark, gorgeous male lead in the South Central shows.

"I'm right here," Erin said, wiggling her orangy fingers at him. "How'd the set hold up?"

"Fine, but Mr. Calvert wants to see you. I think he wants you to cut a door through the rear wall. I need a stupendous door for a dramatic exit," he said, swirling his cape around him.

Maya and I exchanged a smile. Brandon pushed our lunches aside and perched on the table in front of us.

"What's with you girls, holed up in here when the splendor of Café South Central awaits you?"

"Where are the cue cards?" I asked, looking over my shoulder.

"You're Kerri, right?" He zoned in on me. "How do I know you? Didn't we have a class together last year?"

"Math with Ms. Milewski," I said, but I had a feeling Brandon knew who I was. He flirted with me that whole year. Managed to get a seat near me. Always tried to arrange a study session before big tests. Once a week he'd pencil his phone number on the cover of my notebook. And once a week I'd erase it.

"I'm Brandon," he said with a shy smile. "But I bet you don't remember me."

"I might." I smiled back. With the way Matt had me feeling, it was fun to play the flirting game with a guy again, even if it was just a game.

"Let's see." He extended a hand toward me, and I paused, wondering if he wanted to shake. "Go ahead, give me your hand," he said. "I'm harmless."

Maya giggled as I held out my hand to him.

He gripped it like a handshake, and his touch felt warm and soft. Not electric like Matt's but very nice. He placed his other hand over my knuckles and stroked them gently. "Now close your eyes."

I started to laugh, but he shook his head. His green eyes stared into mine intently, seriously. I felt a flicker of warmth as he squeezed my hand gently. "Close your eyes," he almost whispered.

Humoring him, I closed my eyes. "Do you see it? We knew each other in a former life."

I opened my eyes.

"Did you see it?" he asked.

"Yes." I nodded. "We definitely knew each other in a former life, long before Ms. Milewski's math class."

"I knew it," Brandon said. "Where did we meet?"

I laughed again. "We were in Landon's social studies class, back in ninth grade."

Brandon pointed a finger at me. "You're quick. You know, we should get together sometime. Talk the talk. Whatever."

"I don't know. . . ." I was about to tell him I had a boyfriend, but I didn't. I just didn't.

"Like I said, whatever." He jumped off the table and picked up a pen from Mr. Calvert's desk. "Book, please?" he asked.

I smiled and fished out a spiral from my backpack. I opened it to a clean page and handed it to Brandon.

"This time I'm using ink," he said, writing his number. "So you can't erase it."

"This place is packed," Jessica said, descending into the shadows of the Cellar on Saturday night. I followed her down the stairs, trying to ignore the anger burning inside me. It was Friday night, and here I was out with a friend because my so-called boyfriend hadn't even asked if I was coming to see him perform. I was so angry that I couldn't even talk to Jess about it anymore.

Yesterday at school, I'd gotten the same cool brush-off from Matt that I had on Thursday. In the morning he was too busy joking with his buds to pay attention to me. And at lunchtime he ran off to rehearsal again. That quiet, serious jazz musician light was in his eyes, a light I'd always found so attractive, so sexy. But now it just made me mad. Mr. Live-for-the-Moment was leaving me completely out of his moments.

I stomped into the club, determined to grab Matt when he wasn't performing and straighten things out once and for all. He was being mean. He was avoiding me. He needed to apologize and take back everything he'd said about seeing other people and . . . and start loving me again. That was what was missing—the incredible connection between us.

And it was all his fault. How could he be so stupid?

As my eyes adjusted to the shadowy room, I tried to filter out the noise of music, voices, and clinking pool balls. The jukebox was still playing, so Matt's band wasn't performing yet. Behind the keyboards one of the musicians, a guy with spiky hair named John, kept adjusting knobs on the sound system. Still no sight of Matt.

"Do you want to get some Cokes?" Jessica asked me.

"Maybe in a minute," I said. "Do you see Matt?"

I spotted Erin back by the billiards tables,

holding a pool cue. She was talking to Glen, who was just about to take a shot.

"No," Jessica said. "But Maya and Luke saved a table. Let's head over that way."

We moved out from behind the crowd around the juice bar, and there was Matt, standing up, straightening out an extension cord by the band setup. A minute after I spotted him, he saw me. There was a flicker of something in his eyes, but I couldn't decipher it.

How could he not still love me?

I kept my gaze on him as I followed Jess through the crowded room. Two girls came up to Matt. One put her arm on his shoulder. The other was all giggles. I recognized their faces: eleventh-graders. Band groupies. And they had Matt's attention. *Oh, go away!* I wanted to shout.

But they didn't. In fact, Matt seemed to be pretty cozy with them even though he knew I was watching. He was talking to them, making eye contact, and he had a huge smile for the giggler.

What was going on? I grabbed the back of Jess's coat to point out Matt, but when she turned around, it wasn't Jess. I'd grabbed the wrong person—Brandon Slavin.

"Hey, you," he said, turning to touch the sleeve of my jacket. "I like the way you say hello."

"Sorry. I thought you were my friend," I said.

He grinned. "I am."

I turned back to Matt, and my heart dropped to the floor. One of the groupies jumped up and hugged him and he seemed to be loving it! How could he? Right in front of me! Matt glanced over, then quickly looked away. It was like he was trying to hurt me, trying to make me jealous.

Matt turned back to me again, and I felt a frantic impulse to show him that two could play his game. Reaching up, I grabbed Brandon's shoulders to kiss him hello on the cheek.

Brandon quickly turned his face. Our lips met. I gasped as his tongue slid into my mouth.

"Mmm." Brandon slid his arms around my waist.

I pulled away from Brandon and swung back toward Matt.

Matt stared at me, surprised and hurt. And I felt totally awful. I started toward the stage. I had to talk to him.

Matt dropped the electrical cords and shoved his way through the crowd. Not toward me.

"Matt!" I pushed past a couple and tried to squeeze through the wall of people in front of the juice bar.

But he didn't stop. He was heading down a few steps, toward a door that said EMPLOYEES ONLY.

"Wait!" I yelled. I made it to the steps, with Matt just a few feet ahead of me. Breathlessly, I rushed down and reached him just as he put his hand on the door. "Matt, wait."

He turned to me, his eyes dark with total hatred. "Get away," he said.

I watched helplessly as he stormed through the door and slammed it in my face.

Chapter 17

■ stared at the door, not knowing if I should go after him. Things were not supposed to happen this way. Matt was supposed to get a little jealous, not storm out of the club.

And what about him? He was hugging that groupie. Shouldn't I be angry too? I recalled the scene in my mind. The groupie jumped up and hugged Matt. Matt glanced at me. A sick feeling spread through my stomach. Was he hugging the girl back? I wasn't sure anymore. Tears began to stream down my face. Did I misunderstand the whole thing? Did I make Matt jealous for nothing?

I started back up the stairs, then realized I couldn't go back into the main area. I didn't want to be crying in a huge crowd. I rushed up the stairs. Then I cut around the juice bar and ran into the only place of salvation I knew: the ladies' room. Luckily for me, two of the three stalls were empty.

I pushed into one, locked the door, and sat on the toilet and cried. *If our relationship wasn't over before, it definitely is now,* I thought, sobbing. *I ruined everything.*

"Kerri?" I knew that voice. Jessica.

"We know you're in here," Maya said. "She must be in here, right?"

"I'd recognize those boots anywhere," Erin said as I spotted her purple combat boots near the door of my stall. She knocked. "Come on, open up."

I unlocked the door, then sat back and unwound some toilet paper to wipe up my face.

"Ooh, you're a mess," Erin said, peeking in. "Though somehow I'm not surprised."

"What were you doing out there?" Jessica asked, poking her head in.

"I was . . . I was trying to make Matt jealous," I wailed, pressing a ball of toilet paper to my face. "I thought he was flirting with those juniors, and I wanted to see what it would be like if I did that. I thought that when he saw me with Brandon, he'd be so jealous that he'd realize how much he needs me. That we're so right together."

"Well, I'd say that's one plan that backfired," Erin said.

"I really didn't plan it," I said. "And now I'm not even sure if he was flirting in the first place.

That shows you. Spontaneity can kill you."

Jessica reached in and grabbed my arm. "Come on out of there. A line's forming, and that stall is too small for the four of us." She led me to the sinks.

Maya held my hair back while I splashed cold water onto my face.

Straightening up, I blotted my cheeks with a paper towel and then looked in the mirror. My eyes were puffy. My nose was red. "That was a big mistake," I said, taking a deep breath. I felt another sob shake me, and I buried my face in my hands.

"You'll be okay," Jessica said, hugging me.

"It just feels miserable while you're in the miserable part," Erin added. "You try to pull yourself together. I'll go outside and start damage control. If Matt's back, he might be ready to talk. And then there's Brandon. . . ."

"Brandon!" I shook my head. "He thinks I like him. He kissed me on the lips."

"I have a feeling Brandon is hip to everything by now," Erin said, leaning toward the mirror to rake her fingers through the raspberry streak in her hair.

"Could you tell him I'm sorry?" I asked Erin. "I kind of used him."

She nodded and headed out.

"Wait!" I called, and Erin stopped. "I should explain it myself." I looked at the faces of my three best friends. "And then I should probably go home," I added. "I've had enough fun for one night."

I opened my eyes the next morning and stared at the gray sunlight filtering through the blinds. All I could think about was Matt. Was he up yet? Was he angry? Sad? Did he ever go back on stage and perform?

I thought about calling him, but I knew he wouldn't talk to me. Rubbing my eyes, I kicked off the covers and sat up. I could e-mail him an apology. I crawled across the bed, turned on the computer, and rubbed my hands together and yawned. What would I say?

Sorry. Sorry that I kissed another guy in front of you. Sorry that I tried to make you jealous. You see, I was just trying to save our relationship. Yeah, right. That would work.

I was still trying to think of the perfect apology as I logged on and found that I had mail. It was a message from Erin.

> Woke up with a two-ton head. Flu? I don't know, but it's clogging my nose and my brain. Can't do Milwaukee. Sorry. Send chocolates.
> —Erin

Milwaukee! I put my head on the desk with a groan. Maybe I could cancel. I didn't want to go anymore, not after what had happened with Matt last night. My first instinct was to bag the trip and drive over to Matt's house and camp out on his front porch until he agreed to talk to me. No, I decided. My father was expecting me. I kind of felt committed.

But I still didn't want to go alone. I passed Dan's room on the way to the kitchen and stopped. Dad wanted Dan to come along, I remembered. I should have asked him.

I knocked on my brother's door. No answer. Then I opened it. Dan's shades were drawn, and the room was pitch black. My brother was fast asleep under the covers.

"Dan!" I called. "Want to go to Milwaukee with me? To Dad's?"

He rolled over and groaned. "Up late. Close door." He turned around and went back to sleep.

Looks like I'm going alone, I thought. *Why not? I'm seventeen, and I'll be heading off to Miami alone in the fall. Surely I can make the short drive to Milwaukee on my own, right?*

I ate breakfast and took a quick shower. Then I packed everything I needed in my backpack, tossed it onto the passenger seat of my car, and was headed on my way.

Snowflakes danced through the air and whipped past my windshield, but the highway was clear. I turned up an old Smashing Pumpkins song on the radio and started thinking of how to talk to Matt when I get back on Sunday. That should be enough time for him to cool down.

I was on number twelve—hide homemade fudge in his locker—when I realized I'd go crazy if I couldn't get my mind off Matt. I let my mind wander to meeting my father's family. Sandy would be warm and welcoming. And Gabby . . . she'd finally have the big sister she always wanted. Someone to play with, bring her special toys, take her exciting places. Could I be that sister? Did I *want* to be that sister?

As I got closer to Milwaukee, I had to pull myself out of my thoughts to concentrate on the road, which was turning icy. By the time I turned onto Caswell Lane, I was glad to be ending the drive.

The snowstorm was furious now, with white flakes filling the air. Dad's block reminded me of one of those villages in a snow globe as I pulled up to the house and parked in front. And there was Dad opening the front door, completing the scene with the precious, curly-haired blond girl in his arms and the beautiful wife standing beside him.

The picture of domestic bliss.

Suddenly panic gripped me. What was I doing there? Oh, right. I needed that check. And they wanted me there. They were welcoming me. I grabbed my backpack and ducked into the snowstorm.

"Kerri!" Dad called as I tramped through the snow. "Come in, come in! We're so glad you made it." He greeted me warmly, though there was an awkward moment as I stepped inside. I wasn't quite sure if I should kiss him. I would have hugged him, but he had the little girl in his arms.

He ended up giving me a bear hug with Gabby in his arms, which made the little girl complain. "Dad, you're squishing me!"

"Sorry, pumpkin." Dad released me, then brushed the snow off my shoulders playfully. "We've got the fireplace going, and Sandy is going to make you some spiced cider," Dad told me.

"If she likes it," Sandy added. "A lot of kids don't go for cider, Michael."

"But yours is so good," he told his wife. "Would you like some, Kerri?"

"Sure," I said, wondering if they were arguing about me already. I guess I'd also been expecting Dad to introduce all of us, but he was already bounding up the stairs with Gabby in his arms, and she was giggling all the way.

"I'll take your coat," Sandy said, reaching out a slender arm toward me. Her voice was so even and her face so emotionless that I couldn't read her. Was she being polite or trying to keep me from dripping on her carpet?

She was quite delicate. Her curly, light brown hair was swept behind both ears. Very neat. She didn't at all resemble my mother, who liked to wear her hair loose.

I slid off my ski jacket and handed it to her, feeling really uncomfortable. When did my father meet this woman? What did he love about her? She didn't seem like a match for my dad. Very tense. Maybe because I was there.

"Come on, Kerri!" Dad called from the short flight of steps. "We'll show you around. I want you to feel right at home here."

As Sandy tucked my coat into the front closet, I stomped the snow off my boots. Then I climbed the stairs to a large open room with shiny oak floors, Chinese rugs, and brocaded furniture. Photos of Gabby framed in gold and silver were everywhere. No pictures of Dan and me, but I wasn't sure if Dad had any.

"The living room, dining room, kitchen, and bedrooms are on this level," he said. "Though

Gabby and I call this room the museum, since no one does much living in here. Right, Gabby?"

"I'm not allowed to play in here," Gabby said sullenly.

"Oh, too bad," I said, though I could see why. I could just imagine Gabby leaving raisins under the sofa cushions and plastering shiny stickers all over the marble-topped tables. Or maybe that was me when I was five? I was wondering if my parents ever had furniture this nice when Dad moved on.

"The kitchen," he said, pointing to a shiny, modern room with a spotless floor. "Feel free to help yourself anytime. And we have three bedrooms up here."

"Show her mine first!" Gabby ordered, ruffling my father's hair. "Mine first!"

"Of course!" Dad told her. "Princess Gabriella's bedchambers are the grandest in the land." He swept her into a room with pink rosebud wallpaper and gently tossed her onto a pink and white comforter so puffy that I would swear it was made of marshmallows.

"This is really nice, Gabby," I said, trying to sound impressed, which wasn't difficult, since the room looked like the Christmas display at the toy store on State Street. There were shelves and bins loaded with colorful toys, from the complete minikitchenette in the corner to the shelves of elegant dolls dressed in glittering gowns. Watching Gabby pick up a toy, I realized she resembled a doll herself, dressed in a pretty white dress with pink leggings.

"This is Rebecca," Gabby told me, showing me a doll dressed in purple ruffles. "She's going to a party at her friend's house. There's a merry-go-round there. And a clown. And lots of vanilla ice cream."

"Sounds great," I said. "Can I come to the party?"

"Mmm, maybe next time," Gabby answered.

My life story. I'd never had a room like this. When we lived in the house in Kensington Heights, I was too young to care, and then after we moved to the apartment, there was no money for toys or decorating.

Try to get a hold of yourself, I thought. It was too ridiculous for a seventeen-year-old girl to be jealous of a five-year-old. Still, I couldn't help seeing green every time Gabby ran over to hug our father or told me yet another story about yet another one of her dolls. How could she have gotten so much—and so much of him—when I'd been left with so little?

Dad finished the house tour downstairs with a

look at the family room and the guest room where I'd be sleeping. My room was large and had its own bathroom. I washed my face and braced myself for more merging into the perfect family.

Later we sat around the fire and sipped spiced cider in the family room, but Gabby was quickly bored with our conversation and her video. She talked Dad into playing a board game with her, leaving Sandy and me to struggle through a conversation.

"Your father tells me you're a senior in high school," Sandy was saying. "I loved my senior year. All those dances and games and the senior class trip. We went to Washington, D.C."

"Senior year is great," I said. What else was I going to say to this woman? "Um, I don't know where we're going for our senior trip yet." An awkward silence. I glanced at her. Sandy was staring at the fireplace, obviously uncomfortable. "So . . . how did you and my dad meet?" I asked, trying to find common ground.

Sandy's brown eyes almost disappeared as a warm smile spread across her face, a smile that surprised me. "About six years ago I was taking a real estate class, and your father was the teacher."

Six years, I made a mental note. *That was after Mom and Dad divorced.* "Dad's in real estate?" I asked, suddenly realizing that I didn't even know what my father did for a living.

Sandy nodded. "Yes. And he asked me out after our third class. I didn't want to go at first because he was my teacher. But he kept sending me flowers and cards." She paused, smiling. "One time he even hired a guitar player and sang under my window." She started laughing. "He was awful!"

I cracked up with her. "That sounds like something my dad would do."

"It was so corny, I *had* to go out with him!" Sandy added.

"That's a cute story," I said. *And she's not that bad*, I thought, feeling a little guilty for almost liking her.

Then Gabby ran down to replenish her toy supply, and Dad soon followed.

"I guess I should start dinner," Sandy said, and headed upstairs.

Alone with Dad, I decided this was a good time to remind him about one of the reasons I'd come. "Before I forget," I said, "I need the check for the room deposit. It feels so weird owing Jessica that much money."

"Oh, right!" He made a joke of slapping his forehead, then went over to the desk and pulled his checkbook out of a drawer. "Let's see. Pay to the order of Kerri Hopkins. Amount . . . fifteen thousand dollars." I glanced up with a look of disbelief and amazement, and he grinned. "Just kidding. Fifteen hundred, is it?" he asked. "Let me know when the rest of the room and board payment is due," he added. "And I figured I'll give you about three hundred dollars a month for spending money. Does that sound good?"

"Wow," I said, amazed that he wanted to pay for more than just the room and board. "It sounds great!"

"Michael?" Sandy called from the stairs. "Can you come up and give me a hand with this?"

"Sure, honey," he called, dropping his pen into the checkbook. "Be right back."

I stood up and paced by the ceramic tiles of the warm fireplace. Something about the flames was comforting, and I had the feeling that I'd come to the end of a long journey. Not just the journey to the right college but the path to finding my father too. And with a little time, maybe I'd also get to know Sandy and Gabby.

Settling down near the fire, I heard my father and Sandy talking upstairs.

"It's just not right, Michael," she said. "You know we can't afford it, not with the mortgage payments. And what about the lease on the SUV? The bank called me about that twice this week."

"I just forgot about it, really," he said in a quiet voice. "I'll get that out this week."

"From what account?" Sandy asked. "We're overdrawn in checking. And we're maxed out on all of our cards. Honey, you have to be honest with her. We don't have the money to pay our own bills. If we give her as much as you told her, we'll lose the house."

My stomach twisted as my brain worked to process their words. What was going on up there?

"I told her we'd help her," he said, "and we can."

"No," Sandy said emphatically. "Michael, I won't let you jeopardize this house just so you can look good. You need to focus, honey. Think about Gabby and us. We're barely keeping our heads above water as it is."

"I can't," I heard my dad reply.

Their words came down the stairs loud and clear. Dad was living on credit. Overdue bills. Major debts. My father hadn't changed. He was still racing off to get what he wanted, dealing with the reality of those decisions later.

The truth was that Dad didn't have the money. And he and his wife were fighting over me. Even worse, I had just mailed off my life savings, along with Jess's savings. And now I had no way to pay my friend back. What was I going to do?

Someone was coming down the stairs. I froze

in a panic as Sandy entered the family room. Where was my father? Hiding upstairs? Not wanting to face me?

"Kerri, I have to be honest with you. I know your father promised to pay for your college room and board, but it's out of the question."

Even though I'd heard them arguing upstairs, the news seemed so dismal coming from Sandy. "Why did he do that?" I asked. "Why would he make that promise when he had no intention of keeping it?"

"Oh, he had every intention of following through," she said, crossing to the desk to pick up the checkbook. "Your father wants to make you happy, Kerri." She took the pen out of the checkbook and closed it. "But the reality is that we just don't have the money. I'm sorry."

I couldn't look at her. How sorry could she be in this beautiful house filled with beautiful things?

I had to get out of there. I bolted toward the stairs and bounded up the steps two at a time. On the foyer landing I paused long enough to grab my jacket from the closet. My keys were in the right-side pocket. Perfect.

"Kerri?" Sandy called from down below. I ignored her.

A thick layer of snow had covered the front

porch since I'd arrived. Icy snow blew into my face as I trudged down to my car, which was already a white blob in the white landscape. Quickly, I entered the car, turned the defroster on full blast, and brushed off the windows. A minute later I snapped on my seat belt and pulled away.

I drove into the blinding snow, working hard to stay on the road. My car inched along, skidding to a slow stop at the end of the street. I turned onto the main road and tried to sort out all the painful details.

Dad wasn't going to help me. Miami or bust was going to be a bust. I flashed back to those applications to other colleges. Applications that I'd joyfully tossed into the recycle bin this week. I'd missed the admissions deadlines.

Come September, I would be stuck in Madison, living in my old bedroom, just like my brother, Dan. While nearly everyone I knew would be heading off to colleges around the country.

On top of all that, last night I'd totally destroyed my relationship with the only guy I'd ever really loved.

I'd really screwed myself. Big time.

Suddenly I lost the road for a frantic second. I lifted my foot from the gas pedal, searching for it. It was so hard to tell in the thick, blowing snow. Spotting a sign on the roadside ahead, I managed to figure out where the road should be. My car pressed on, the only vehicle in sight, though my sight was so limited that that didn't mean much.

I was sorry I'd ever gotten in touch with my father. That was my big mistake. Actually, why was I blaming myself?

He hadn't changed all that much. Wasn't that why he had stayed away all those years? I remembered something Mom had said about him. "Michael hates not being the hero in Kerri's life," she once told my grandmother when she thought I couldn't hear her. "He can't stand to look bad, to have people think of him as the father who walked out."

So instead, he moved away—*stayed away*—and started another family where he could be the shining star. My dad was definitely an all-or-nothing kind of guy. I could see that so clearly now. If his charisma couldn't cover up a difficult situation, he pretended that it didn't exist.

The car hit a bump under the snow. My hands flew off the steering wheel. I grabbed the wheel so hard, my hands shook. I tried to brake, but I was sliding, skidding fast into the blur of white.

I screamed as the car spun out of control!

Chapter 18

I held tight to the steering wheel as the car skidded. Next came a loud scraping sound and a hollow bang. My head jerked forward and almost smacked the steering wheel.

Then there was silence.

I closed my eyes. I was shaking all over.

I took a deep breath and realized I was okay. My seat belt had kept me in place, and nothing felt sore. I opened my eyes and glanced in the rearview mirror. No cuts or bruises on my face. I was lucky.

Now if I could just get out of the car. The passenger door was flat up against a wall of snow. I knew it wouldn't open, and the driver's-side door had a tendency to stick shut. I banged it twice, then pushed my shoulder against it as I turned the handle. I wiggled out of the car and managed to climb out onto the shoulder of the road.

Wind whipped my hair as I surveyed the

damage. I'd driven into a ditch. And my poor car wasn't going anywhere at the moment.

Still shaking, I turned back toward the road and shielded my eyes against the biting snow. Just behind me I could make out odd shapes covered in white. Monkey bars . . . a kids' playground. The elementary school, I realized. The WAWA should be just ahead. Zipping my ski jacket up to my chin, I lowered my head and tramped through the heavy snow.

My ski jacket was warm enough, but my head was bare and snow stuck to my hair and stung my face. When I reached the snowy parking lot of the WAWA, I yanked the door open and stepped inside to a blast of warm air and rock music. I stamped my feet on the little red rug by the door and brushed the clingy snow out of my hair.

"Whoa, a brave one!" the guy behind the counter told me. "I haven't had a customer here for like, an hour."

"It's pretty wicked out there," I said, unable to get rid of the shakes.

"I was thinking of closing. Either that or I'm stuck here all night." He turned toward the glass case by the wall. "Well, if I'm snowed in, at least I've got plenty of milk."

I wondered if I was going to be stuck there with him. "Right," I said, searching my pockets for my wallet. "Where's your phone?"

He pointed toward the corner near the window. As I went down the aisle, I realized my backpack with my wallet inside it was safe on the bed in Dad's guest room. The best I could come up with was forty-two cents and a piece of lint, but I did know the number of Mom's calling card. "For emergencies only," she always told me. I figured this qualified.

I picked up the phone and watched as my trembling fingers punched in my home number. Busy. Dan must be online. Maybe Mom was on the phone.

I called Jessica, and her mother answered. "She's on her way home from campus. I hope the car doesn't get stuck in the snow," Mrs. Carvelli said. "Do you want her to call you?"

"No," I said hesitantly. It would only freak Jess's mom out if I explained that I was snowbound in a WAWA outside Milwaukee. "I'll call her later. Thanks."

I knew that Maya wouldn't be able to help me, and Erin was too sick. Who else could I call?

Matt. He was furious with me. Probably not speaking to me. But under these horrible circumstances, wouldn't he be a big enough guy to put his anger aside? I punched in his number.

I was just about to tap in the numbers of the calling card when the WAWA's door opened and snow blew in, along with my father. He had followed me even in a blinding snowstorm. Wasn't that just the sort of dramatic rescue he would go for? He thrived on stuff like this.

"Kerri!" He swung toward me, his face full of concern and relief as he came down the aisle. "Are you okay? I saw your car and . . . are you hurt?"

"I'm fine," I said, hanging up the phone with a shiver. "Just perfect."

He came closer, then paused. "We were so worried. I was worried. Honey, I'm sorry about everything. Come on back to the house with me. We'll work things out."

I folded my arms across my chest and frowned. It was the last place on earth I wanted to be. Okay, the second-to-last place, right behind the freezing cold snowstorm. But I realized that I didn't have much choice. Even if I did get through to someone in Madison, there was no way they could drive through this storm to rescue me. It was either spend the night at Dad's house or stay at the WAWA.

"Please?" he added.

Staring down at the ground, I followed him out to his car. I climbed in and slammed the door behind me. As Dad put the vehicle in gear, I could see it was much easier to manage in the snow with four-wheel drive. I sighed as we passed my disabled car.

"I'm sure we can get a tow truck to pull you out in the morning," Dad said. "Hopefully, there's no major damage."

"It's an old car," I said sullenly. *Not like this squeaky new SUV.*

"I'm so glad you're safe," Dad said. "We'll be home in a snap, then we'll warm you up with some blankets and a nice hot—"

"Just stop, okay?" I interrupted him. I hugged myself, still shaking inside. "I am not going to let you play the hero in all this."

"What?" He sounded confused.

"The way you have to play Superdad, the great rescuer. The guy who saves the day and steals the show at every party and picnic. Well, it's not working for you anymore, okay? You really hurt me with your big act. I mean, I would have rather you just be a normal guy who came around to visit instead of someone bigger than life who's never there. Do you know how much you hurt Dan and me? Do you have any idea?"

"I'm sorry. Really."

"No, don't give me that line," I said. "It's no excuse for lying. You should have been honest with me. You should have told me that you couldn't afford to help me with college. But no, you made up this huge lie. What was that about? Were you trying to buy my acceptance?"

"No! I was . . ." He let out a breath and turned back to the white road. He slowed to make the turn onto Caswell Lane, and I watched him, waiting for an answer. I wasn't going to let him off the hook.

"Kerri, I know I've made a lot of mistakes when it comes to you. I honestly don't know how to begin fixing our relationship. Maybe that's something I'm just not good at. But I do know that I want to fix it."

I shook my head. "It's way beyond that point, Dad."

He pulled into the driveway and put the brake on. "Don't say that, honey."

But I was already out of the SUV, slipping across the driveway. I saw Sandy standing behind the glass storm door. She'd been waiting for us, probably worried. Well, she could worry all night for all I cared.

"We're back," I said, walking past her. Then, without taking a minute to brush off the snow, I went downstairs and marched right into the guest room, slamming the door behind me.

Once I got out of my jacket and boots, I realized I wasn't shaking anymore. In fact, I felt surprisingly calm.

I stood at the floor-to-ceiling window and watched the snow falling over the surrounding backyards. Funny, I thought, how snow can cover things, make them seem so pure and glittery, when underneath there are a million bumps and snags.

I was so hurt and disappointed in my father—and in myself. Who'd believe I could be such an idiot? I'd trusted my college future to the father who had never been there for me, so why had I expected that he'd be there now? And through it all Mom had tried to help with her "safety school" speeches. Why hadn't I listened to her? Despite her flaky appearance, she was the one who always steered me right.

I had to talk to her. I picked up the phone and sat on the thick rug in front of the window. I dialed, hoping to get through this time.

"Hello?" Mom answered, and it felt so good to hear her voice.

"It's me," I said, still staring out at the snow. "And I've screwed up, big time." I told her about the car accident, which prompted a zillion questions, mostly to make sure that I was okay. Then I told her that Dad wasn't coming through with the money. I even told her that I hadn't applied to any other colleges.

"Oh, Kerri," she said. "None of this matters as

long as you're okay. Let's not worry about school right now. Things have a way of working out. If it's in the stars, it will happen. But I'm so sorry that your father hurt you again."

I didn't reply. I was just glad that she wasn't saying, "I told you so."

"You know," Mom continued, "I hoped that your father had learned a few things over the years. But it must have been a difficult time for him. I can't imagine how it felt for him, living without his children."

I frowned. "You think that bothered him?"

"It must have crushed him," Mom said. "Personally, I couldn't have survived without you and Dan in my life. I know I'm not one of those TV moms, but the thought of you two growing up without me is unbearable."

That struck me. "I always thought that you were just stuck with Dan and me. You can't tell me you were happy being a single parent with two kids. Wasn't that why you were always taking classes and studying Buddhism?"

"What?" Mom asked.

"I thought you wanted to get away from us. You know, emotional escape."

Mom's laughter rang through the phone line. "Oh, honey. I did all those things to be a better person, a better mother to you kids. There's a big difference."

"I guess there is," I said, wondering why I'd never seen my mother clearly.

After I hung up, I felt a twinge of guilt. I'd always been sort of negative about my family, quick to dismiss Mom and Dan. But as I stretched out on the bed, I realized I did have a family. A loving family, even if it didn't resemble the families on television.

I wondered if my family would ever grow to include my father. It was hard to say.

Just then there was a knock on the door. "Kerri, are you in there?" Gabby called. "Dad says dinner is ready. I'm having mac and cheese, but you're having roast beast. Do you like roast beast?"

"I'll be there in a minute," I called, and tried to collect myself. When I opened the door, I was startled to find Gabby still standing there, holding a doll with pretty black hair and a blue dress.

She held it out to me. "You can play with Bambi tonight."

She looked so cute with her big curls that I had to smile. "Thanks!" I said, and took the doll. "Hey! Race you up the stairs?"

She ran ahead of me, giggling. "I won, I won!" she cried at the top of the stairs.

Dad put a bowl of mashed potatoes on the table and smiled at me. "I knew Gabby would get you out of your room."

I didn't smile back. I wanted to keep the peace, but I wasn't going to pretend things were perfect. "Yup," I said, sitting down at the table. "She twisted my arm."

"Gabby! I told you to stop that arm twisting!" Dad joked.

"I didn't do it!" Gabby exclaimed, crouching behind her plate of cheesy orange noodles.

"I know you didn't." Dad hugged her, then tweaked her nose. "Got your nose!"

Oh, not that old joke, I thought as I scooped a spoonful of potatoes onto my plate. Dad was really pouring on the jokes tonight, like a little kid trying to distract a parent from his bad behavior.

Suddenly I saw myself in our old kitchen in Kensington Heights. I was probably Gabby's age, and I'd just spilled a full glass of milk on the floor. I knew my parents would be angry, so I defused the whole situation by breaking into a dance routine, a sort of hopping set of moves my father had taught me.

Now, watching Dad ham it up at the dinner table, it hit me. In some ways I was just like him.

Chapter 19

The next morning I was on the phone updating Jessica when I saw a tow truck pull up outside with my car dangling from the back. "There's my car," I said, peering out the window.

"How's it look?" Jessica asked.

"A little scraped and dented, but that's nothing new. At least it runs. The mechanic called Dad earlier to say everything checked out." Dad, who had been outside clearing the driveway with a snow blower, was talking with the tow truck driver. I pulled on my jacket. "I'd better go."

"Call me as soon as you get home," Jessica ordered.

"Okay, 'bye!" I grabbed my backpack and dashed outside.

The driver was already lowering my car to the street, which had been plowed that morning. The wind had died down, and sunlight sparkled over the clean white snow. On the lawn there were two snow angels and the beginnings of a snowman Dad and Gabby had started earlier.

"Your chariot awaits," Dad called, leaning on my car. "I took care of the tow and the mechanic's bill. You're all set."

"Thanks," I said, wondering how Sandy felt about that. She seemed to be the one who clamped down on family spending.

"Well, I guess I'd better get going," I said, hitching my backpack onto my shoulder.

"Wait, just a second," Dad said. He went into the house. A moment later he returned with Sandy, who was bundled up in a jacket. "Before you go," Dad said, "we wanted to at least give you this." He handed me an envelope.

I opened the flap. There was a check inside for five hundred dollars.

"Please don't hate me," Dad said. "That's the best we can do right now."

I looked from him to Sandy, who nodded her approval like a nervous mom.

The old Kerri would have torn his check to pieces. But not the new Kerri. I closed the envelope and tucked it into my backpack. At least I would be able to pay Jessica back.

"You know," I said, "I don't hate you, Dad. I just

don't know what kind of relationship we can have. Without honesty and trust. With your new family . . ." I shrugged. "I just don't know."

He touched my chin and then my hair. His eyes twinkled in that familiar, charming way. "Still, I'm your father. You're stuck with me. And I'd like to try. So that check is just an installment. It's time for me to pay child support for you, at least until you turn eighteen. It may not amount to a lot in terms of college, but I'll send you a check like that whenever I can."

Less than a year of child support. It wasn't much. Was it more than he could afford? I looked over at Sandy, who nodded again.

"As much as we can," she said. "I'll make it happen."

Wonders never cease, I thought as I got into my car. The money would help. But I'd heard that "the check's in the mail" line from Dad before. And I wasn't about to go through the courts to make him pay. Mom, Dan, and I had survived this long without his help.

As I drove back to Madison, I conjured up new and exciting ways to come up with enough money to pay my college bill. As soon as I got back, I was going to give Dan ten dollars for ten more lottery tickets. And what about those TV game shows for teens? I was going to start calling that 800 number that night. Even if I just made it to the finals, there was big prize money involved. And there was always a student loan.

It was just after noon when I reached the outskirts of Madison. At a traffic light I turned away from home, toward the center of town. I knew that Matt would be with his friends, rehearsing for tonight's performance. The Cellar. My stomach felt tight.

This was not going to be fun.

Guitar music ripped through the air as I opened the door to the Cellar. The club wasn't open yet, and chairs were still stacked on the tables. Across the room Larry stood against the brick wall, thumbing his bass guitar. John leaned over his keyboards, his spiky hair looking a little flat this afternoon. Matt stared at the floor as he worked through the song.

Hey, everybody, the jerk is here! I wanted to yell. But I figured I was in enough trouble without interrupting their rehearsal.

I sat on a table, and suddenly Matt looked up. He wasn't happy to see me. He closed his eyes and wailed on the guitar.

When the song was over, I clapped.

Matt glared at me, but John and Larry seemed to appreciate it. Matt unplugged his guitar and stormed over. "What are you doing here?"

"I have to apologize," I said. I'd been calm so far, but now I felt tears stinging my eyes. "I am so sorry about the scene with Brandon. It was mean—I know it was. But I was so mad that you wanted to see other people."

Matt shook his head. "This was never about seeing other people. That's not what I want. I just need some space sometimes. I'm crazy about you, Kerri, but you can be such a bulldozer, planning out everything and assuming everyone is along for the ride."

"And you didn't like the ride?" I asked him.

"People need choices." He sat down beside me and picked out a few notes on the guitar. "I mean, you didn't even listen when I tried to explain about Purdue. My parents weren't listening either. But I put my foot down. I'm not going. I'm sick of following along."

"Really?" I was surprised. "What are you going to do?"

"Go to Boston College, if I get in. And I'm not playing football. They've got a great music program. My parents are pissed, but they'll get over it. In like, a hundred years."

"That's great," I said. "My news isn't so good. I might not be going to Miami after all." I explained how everything had wound down with my dad.

He stopped playing to listen. "I'm sorry to hear that. I know how much you're into Miami."

I nodded. "But I'll work something out. You know me, always planning." I smiled at him. He didn't smile back. "Oh, Matt," I said, my voice cracking with emotion. "The important thing is us. Do you forgive me?"

He shrugged. "What you did was pretty awful. I need some time to think about it, you know?"

I felt a twinge of panic. It wasn't the answer I wanted to hear. But instead of pushing, I bit my lip. *Just zip it,* I told myself. *Matt said he needs space.*

"Hey, Matt," Larry called. "Let's go."

As Matt got up to join the other two musicians, I sat there, lips zipped, feeling totally rejected. I held a huge sob in my throat as the guys began another song. I was going to burst into tears right there, in front of Matt and the guys in the band. I pressed a finger into my temple. *Don't cry, don't cry, don't cry!*

I swallowed hard, trying to let the bad feelings slip out of my body and leave room for the good feelings to come in. It was one of my mother's meditation exercises, and at least it made me feel a sense of calm. Focus on the music, I thought as Matt looked up from his guitar.

My heart lifted. The longing in his eyes. I could feel the electricity sparking between us. It was that breathless, tugging force between us that made our relationship so special. How could he not feel it too?

Just then a shaft of light shot through the room as Erin stepped in. She came straight over to me. "Jessica told me you'd be here," she whispered, perching beside me on the table. "It was the last thing she said before I hung up on her. I swear, I am never calling that girl again."

"What?" I turned to her. "What happened now?"

"It's the same old thing." She nodded toward Matt. "How'd it go?"

"Awful." That quivery sad feeling was back. "I talked to him, but he doesn't know if we can get past this."

"Oh, come on," Erin said, looking from me to Matt. "You guys have such a strong chemistry, it's heating up this whole room! He'd have to be dead not to feel it."

"Maybe he can feel it, but he still can't forgive me."

"Nah. You guys are destined to be together." She threw an arm around my shoulders and gave me a squeeze. "You know, I finally looked at that astrology book your mom loaned me. You and Matt, Virgo and Pisces. It says you're perfect together. It's fate. It'll definitely work out." She listened to the music, then nodded. "Matt just doesn't know it yet."

I watched him strum a mellow chord, his eyes smoky and distant and intense as he stared off into the shadows. I felt myself falling in love with him all over again. *Maybe Erin is right,* I thought. *Maybe we're destined to be together.*

TURNING
seventeen #6

This Boy Is Mine
Jessica's Story

"You know what all this perfect, pure white snow makes me want to do?" Glen asked me.

"What?"

"Make snow angels."

I said, "Yeah, me too," before I realized he was kidding.

He burst out laughing.

I gave him a shove. "Let's see some snow angels!"

Glen saluted. He sprawled on his back, spread his arms and legs and made a great snow angel. Next I made one. Then we both got up to inspect our work.

"I don't get 'angel' when I look at yours," I told him. "It seems a little edgy and freakish."

"Freakish!" he echoed. "Take that back."

"No," I said, laughing.

"Take it back," he warned, bending down and scooping some snow into his glove.

"No way!" I turned and grabbed a handful of snow too. I started packing it just as he let the first snowball sail toward my back.

Plunk.

"You're dead, Daley!" I squealed, and took aim.

We chased each other down the street, laughing and throwing snowballs. I dodged a well-aimed one, but lost my balance. The next thing I knew, I was on the ground. Glen tripped over me and landed beside me.

There we were, breathless, laughing, our arms and legs tangled. And as I looked into his face just inches next to mine, I did something incredibly bold and daring. Something I never ever imagined I'd do.

I leaned over and kissed him.